The Rain Catchers

The Rain Catchers

Jean Thesman

Houghton Mifflin Company
Boston   1991

Library of Congress Cataloging-in-Publication Data

Thesman, Jean.

The rain catchers / Jean Thesman.

p. cm.

Summary: Growing up in a house full of women, fourteen-year-old
Grayling learns to deal with death, love, and the unanswered
questions raised by her widowed mother's apparent abandonment.

ISBN 0-395-55333-4

[1. Mothers and daughters — Fiction.   2. Abandoned children —
Fiction.]   I. Title.

PZ7.T3525Rai   1991   90-39343

[Fic]—dc20   CIP

                           AC

Printed in the United States of America

AGM 10 9 8 7 6 5 4 3 2 1

To Barbara and Roy Jones,
of San Diego,
for their help and hospitality;

To Merritt Green and Rob Thesman,
for introducing me to San Francisco.

The Rain Catchers

❧ Chapter 1 ❧

"If I died," Colleen says, her voice dreamy, "if a buffalo ran over me or I fell off a mountain, would you tell my father how much I hated him?"

I'm brushing dog hair off my skirt and I look sideways at her. Her dark head is tipped against the back of the porch swing and her eyes are shut.

"I'd tell him," I say, laughing. "But I wish you'd write him a long letter instead. I could read it aloud at your funeral."

She nods. "You're a good old best pal, Gray. How many summers have we sat on this porch, waiting for teatime, or a honeysuckle rain, or something exciting to happen?"

"Fourteen," I say. "Grandmother has a snapshot of us when we were babies. We were here on the swing, drooling on each other."

Muffled laughter comes from the porch roof and paint chips shower down on the railing. Without opening her eyes, Colleen reaches for my hand and squeezes it. She's giggling.

"Hush," I warn her. "He already thinks we're crazy."

We fall silent, almost drowsy. It's nearly four o'clock on a hot June afternoon at my grandmother's house. We're waiting again for teatime, and a honeysuckle rain, and for something exciting to happen to us.

My grandmother's clocks have no hands. She snapped them off long ago, but she won't tell me why. "Find out for yourself," she says when I coax her for an answer.

So the clocks seem blind, even though hands are not the same as eyes. Still, they know the time. Downstairs in the entrance hall, the grandfather clock bongs out the hours like a jovial giant. From the dining room, the small gilt and rose-colored marble clock on the buffet tinkles a worried echo of the shout from the hall.

Upstairs, everyone's bedroom has a clock with hands except Grandmother's. We all wear watches, too. Grandmother doesn't mind if we need to know the exact time. I think she feels sorry for us.

"Is it going to rain?" Colleen asks me.

"It will rain before dinner," I say. "Stop worrying."

She worries anyway. "I hope you're right. I've got to be home for dinner tonight. *She* says so."

She is Colleen's newest stepmother. This one, Fawn, is twenty-three, nine years older than we are. We enjoy despising her. She looks anorexic and her hair always smells like stale cologne. I think of that now because Colleen and I — and all the women in the house — are waiting for the first honeysuckle rain of the summer. If we collect enough, we'll use it for a final rinse on our hair tonight.

The porch extends across the front of the house and down the side, where we wait. Thirty feet away across the lawn sits the little summer kitchen, its roof and lattice sides covered with blooming honeysuckle. The roof has no gutters, so during summer storms honeysuckle-scented rain drips from the eaves. This is enchanted water, good for house plants and for rinsing one's hair and prettiest underwear. Tomorrow we'll all smell of honeysuckle.

The clock in the hall bongs four times, immediately followed by a tinkling echo from the dining room on the other side of the window next to our swing. A chair scrapes and the tea cart rattles along the passage from the kitchen.

"Oh, tea, thank heaven," my great-aunt, Minette Minor, says in the dining room. "Garnet, do you want help?"

"No, no, sister," Grandmother says. "I've got it." I hear china cups clatter in their saucers.

"At last," Colleen says. "I'm thirsty."

A hand reaches through the white lace curtain at the window and passes a glass of lemonade to Colleen, then reappears with one for me. Raspberries are floating in the lemonade.

"Cookies, too?" Minette asks from behind the curtain.

"Please." Colleen sips from her glass, then reaches for the plate that appears between the lace panels.

"Should I call the boy down?" Minette asks.

The boy is on the porch roof above our heads, scraping paint. He's been working here since school let out two weeks ago, such a fixture now that I hardly notice him.

That's not true. I *pretend* that I don't notice him.

"I'll tell him tea's ready," I say, and I put my glass down on the bench we use as a table out here on the porch in summer. The rest of the year Colleen and I have our tea in the kitchen. The dining room is for the grown-ups.

I know Aaron's heard the call for tea, because the sounds of scraping have slowed. Still, I hang out over the porch railing and call, "Aaron, tea or lemonade?"

"Lemonade," he says, his voice gruff. He adds, "Thank you."

When I return to the swing, Colleen nudges me. Her face is crooked with suppressed laughter.

"Shut up," I whisper. I know I'm blushing.

Belle Russell's car slips around the side of the house just then and stops in front of the steps.

"How come you're so late getting home?" I ask when she reaches the porch. Her black face is slick with perspiration. She won't have air-conditioning in her car because it harms the ozone layer, so the drive home from the hospital must have been awful.

She wipes her forehead with the back of one hand twisted with arthritis. "One consultation turned into three," she says. "Colleen, baby, I saw your father at the hospital."

Colleen scowls. "Did he say anything about me?"

Belle laughs. "Now what do you think? He said that if you were here, I was to tell you to go home. It's their anniversary."

"Screw him," Colleen mutters.

"Not me, I can't stand the man," Belle says with another bark of laughter. She is outrageous, and we are shocked and delighted. She limps in and the screen door slams behind her.

Nobody here likes Dr. Clement. He rents his offices from Grandmother and fusses about everything. And he's mean to Colleen. Really mean.

Aaron Ripley climbs down the ladder propped at the end of the porch roof. His light blue eyes find me and he smiles a little. He's a few inches taller than I, and his brown hair is several shades lighter than mine. And straight.

I lean back toward the open window. "Aaron's down now. He wants lemonade."

Grandmother's hand comes through the curtain, first with lemonade and then with a plate of cookies. I give them to Aaron.

As usual, he won't sit with us, although there are four chairs opposite the swing. He sits on the steps, his back to us, and he studies the summer kitchen and the dollhouse beyond it.

The dollhouse never was a dollhouse. When Grandmother and her sister, Minette, were children, it was their playhouse. For years afterward it was filled with junk that was too shabby for the third floor of the house, where Great-grandmother's maids slept, and too good to throw out. Then Minette's daughter, Yolande, came here to live after her divorce. She writes children's books and she uses the dollhouse as an office.

"Does Yolande know that tea's on?" I call through the window. Yolande is in the middle of a book and forgets everything.

"I buzzed her on the intercom," Grandmother says. "She buzzed back so she's coming." A spoon rings against the edge of a cup. Grandmother says, "Ah, Olivia. You're downstairs. Good for you."

Olivia Thorpe is Grandmother's cousin, and she lives with us, too. She only comes down for tea on her good days.

"How's tricks, Olivia?" Belle asks.

"Fine, fine," Olivia says, her voice faint and trembling. "I hate to bother you, dear, but my happy pills are almost gone. Did you have time to see Dr. Roderick?"

Something clicks on the table. "He sent these. He asks that you come in again next week, though. Not to worry. It's just a little checkup."

"Garnet, give me plenty of sugar," Olivia says to

Grandmother. She laughs. "Sugar can't hurt me now."

"Sugar's *good* for you," Belle says.

Of course she doesn't mean that, but even Colleen and I know that Olivia is dying — and Belle is a loving doctor. I should know. She was my pediatrician until arthritis ruined her.

"You don't have to go home," I whisper to Colleen. "After all, what's your dad going to do?"

She makes a face. "He could give your family a hard time."

I laugh. "If he messes with Grandmother, she'll evict him."

But Colleen is afraid of her father, and it isn't possible for her to understand that someone like Garnet Waverly Templeton flicks away the Dr. Clements of the world like bugs.

Olivia calls through the window, "Girls, will it rain?"

"Absolutely," I say. "Before dinner. The sky looks thick and it's hanging low over the poplars, so it'll rain hard."

Aaron turns toward me, curious. "You all sound like you're glad it's going to rain."

"We are, we are!" Colleen cries, jiggling around on the swing so that my lemonade almost spills.

"I don't see why," Aaron says.

"You're almost done for the day," I say, "and tomorrow's Saturday, so why do you care if the house is wet or not?" I'm feeling sassy and trying hard to keep him from thinking that I care one way or the other about him.

"I was coming back tomorrow," he says. "With Dad laid up, this job's going to take all summer." He's always so careful and earnest when you ask him a question.

"How's your father, Aaron?" Grandmother calls through the window. "I tried phoning this morning but he didn't answer."

"He was probably out walking," Aaron tells her, acting as if it doesn't bother him one bit to carry on a conversation with someone he can't even see. "He's supposed to walk for an hour every morning and every afternoon. But he was fine when I went home for lunch."

Aaron's father had surgery in May and he won't be able to work for another month at least, so Aaron is painting the house, the dollhouse, and the summer kitchen all by himself.

Yolande bolts from the dollhouse with the dogs following her. "Sorry, sorry," she says, hurrying past us and going on inside. The screen door slams. "I was in the middle of something," I hear her tell Grandmother.

The three dogs greet Aaron as if they hadn't seen him earlier in the day. Ben, the Great Dane, makes mooing sounds in Aaron's ear. Markie, the poodle, sees Colleen and pitter-pats over to her. Gip, an ancient mongrel, bats at the screen door until it bounces open far enough to allow him to scoot inside. He knows it's teatime, and there are always leftover cookies.

Everybody's here. Everybody who counts, that is. Inside, Grandmother pours second cups of tea for everyone and the conversation begins. They tell and retell their experiences, which sound almost like stories, because most have beginnings and middles and ends. They've been told so many times that they've taken on a logic real life never has when we struggle with it as it happens.

"This heat reminds me of the summer Rowena died," Olivia says. Rowena was her daughter, who died in Oregon when she was four. "We didn't have rain for thirty-seven days. I'd soak a towel in ice water and hang it over the fan to cool her down."

"I remember that summer," Grandmother says. "Norah got a concussion and cut her lip falling down the porch steps. The scar still shows."

Norah is my mother. I never noticed the scar. But then, I seldom see her. She only visits at Christmas.

Colleen leans toward the window. "Mrs. Templeton, didn't you say you put milkweed on the scar to make it go away?" she calls out. She's heard the story of Norah's fall many times.

"I did, yes," Grandmother calls back.

"Milkweed wouldn't do it," Minette says. "Would it, Belle?"

"Nothing surprises me," Belle says. "My mother removed warts by rubbing pennies on them."

"Norah fell two days before Rowena got sick," Grandmother says. "And then Yolande stepped on the nail and ended up in the hospital with a terrible infection."

"All three of our girls were in the hospital at the same time," Minette says. "They say bad luck comes in threes."

"I shouldn't believe that but I do," Belle says. "Warm this up for me, Garnet. Half a cup is plenty."

"It's like when John's father died," Olivia says, sighing. "Who could have predicted how things would turn out after Jacob Jordan went to his reward?"

They have begun telling my story. Mine is one that doesn't have an ending. When I was small this didn't bother me. Now it does. I'm like a book that was lost before the reader could finish it.

"I'd only been back in Seattle a few months when we heard that Jacob died," Minette says. "And John brought Norah and Gray here from San Diego for a long visit before moving to San Francisco to take over the business."

"I'll never get over how John died," Olivia says, carrying on the story. "Run down in that parking lot by the man who'd just robbed the store. Terrible."

"Then," Minette says, picking up the loose thread of the tale and describing the third disaster, "a few months later Norah left baby Grayling here and went to San Francisco without a word of explanation."

"Strange, so strange," Olivia says. "She'd gone out the night before. I remember that. And she didn't get home until the next morning, covered with mud."

"And her car was gone," Minette adds.

"Well, it was only a rental car," Grandmother says.

"I suppose someone turned it in." This is a small detail, but everything must be accurate during teatime.

There is the usual small pause at this point, while we who know the story so well contemplate my mother's unexplained flight from Seattle. Aaron is staring at me. This is the first time he's heard the story, and he's shocked.

"I still wonder why she left," Grandmother says. She is quiet and resigned — the story's been repeated so many times that it doesn't hurt her now.

Is that why they repeat it and all the other tales of death and abandonment, illness, divorce? Does the telling of it render the past powerless for them?

Aaron, aware that he's been staring, looks away from me.

Suddenly, without the usual scatter of warning drops, the clouds give way and rain pours down, a true honeysuckle rain.

"It's started!" Colleen shouts, leaping to her feet.

I run to follow her, brushing against Aaron in my haste and tingling from the contact like a wind chime.

Colleen ducks under the curtain of honeysuckle that hangs over the summer kitchen door. Before I get there, I hear her dragging the box filled with bottles and jars that are older than we are. They clink against each other as she staggers out with them.

Colleen crouches beside the outside wall of the summer kitchen fireplace, looking upward, trying to judge where the first trickle will appear. Deciding, she twists an olive bottle into the dirt to give it a footing and scrambles back for another. Rain is dripping off the roof now in dozens of places. I shove a fat pickle jar under a large drip, an applesauce jar under a smaller one that may last longer.

"What are you doing?" Aaron is standing over me.

The box is nearly empty, and most of the big drops are falling into jars. The rainwater *plinks* and *plonks* musically. Thunder rolls somewhere east of us and wind stirs my hair. The air is heavy with sweet scent. "We're catching the rain," I say.

"What for?" Aaron asks.

Colleen gets to her feet awkwardly, wiping water from her face. "We use it." She tells Aaron how.

I remember the day Aaron first came to work on the house. "Is this a boarding house?" he asked. He was puzzled by the number of women living here.

"Not exactly," I said. I couldn't explain Grandmother's house to him — there was no way to describe what we have here.

Everyone pays Grandmother a small amount for food. My mother sends regular checks to cover my expenses. But this isn't a boarding house. It's my grandmother's house, where we are safe, where the honeysuckle rain falls in the summer, where most stories have beginnings, middles, and ends.

Yolande, her long brown hair coming loose from her bun, runs out to check the jars, then scurries back to the porch to watch the rain fall. She stands near her mother, who is Minette Waverly Minor; and her aunt, who is my grandmother Garnet Waverly Templeton; and Olivia Thorpe, their cousin who is dying; and Belle Russell, who came as a nurse to care for Grandfather, stayed on while Grandmother put her through medical school, and still lives here as our friend. They watch over one another and everyone watches over me. And Colleen, too. I'm not sure anyone could understand.

Later, when the rain is slackening off, a car charges up the driveway. Dr. Clement leaps out of it and runs across the lawn, shouting at Colleen. Without a word or glance at the rest of us, he grabs her arm and drags her back toward the car.

"What the hell's wrong with you?" he yells. "Can't you follow the simplest instructions? I told you to stay home this afternoon and help your stepmother. You're supposed to do as you're told."

"Paul Clement, let go of that girl!" Grandmother roars from the porch. The dogs are barking from the safety of the doorway.

But Dr. Clement shoves Colleen into the car. He climbs in himself without a word to Grandmother and careens backward down the driveway.

Grandmother is furious. "I won't forget that his lease is up at the end of the year," she says, her voice tight and hard.

"Throw him out on his ass," Belle says, laughing. She hobbles into the house, letting the screen door bang.

"Aroooop!" Ben, the Great Dane, bellows after the car.

"Who was that?" Aaron asks as the car screeches into the street.

"Nobody who matters," I grumble.

The first honeysuckle rain is letting up. Everyone goes inside but Aaron and me. I sit on the swing, he sits on the steps. The clocks announce the time.

Grandmother, at the door once more, says, "We'll see you Monday, Aaron. Tell your father to take care."

Aaron leaves, with a sweet smile for me, and he sprints off toward the truck parked in front of the house.

All my nerve endings have curled up. Minette said bad luck comes in threes. Colleen's problems with her father are reaching a crisis. Olivia is dying. What more can go wrong?

❧ Chapter 2 ❧

A Saturday morning sounds different from other mornings. At six-thirty I'm awake, listening to birds and to the ripple of barking that starts each morning with a dog blocks away and will end here when a boy tosses the paper on the porch and our dogs protest. But on weekdays I'd hear the sounds of cars by now.

Grandmother's house sits in the middle of several acres on a quiet road, next to an abandoned tree farm on the north that grew into a forest. Grandmother bought the tree farm ten years ago to keep developers away. On the other side of the woods a highway leads to Seattle. We pretend it isn't there, but on weekdays we hear the hiss of endless tires, like a distant, threatening surf.

The Great Dane, Ben, sleeps in my room, sometimes on my bed, and he raises his head now, listening to a dog at the south end of the road.

"Don't bark," I tell Ben. He looks at me from the corner of his dark eyes. "You'll wake Olivia."

But Olivia is already awake, I realize. I hear Belle leaving her bedroom across the hall and shuffling next door to Olivia's room. I throw back the covers and fly to my door, which stands open so that Ben can come and go as he pleases. I see Belle's broad back disappear into Olivia's room, and at the same time I hear Olivia whimper breathlessly, "Oh, Belle, bless you."

Belle was carrying a small bottle and a disposable hypodermic needle. Olivia's happy pills must not be working very well again.

I lean against the wall. The bottom has dropped out of my stomach. Belle makes this trip to Olivia's room nearly every morning now. Olivia won't live much longer.

"No, no," I whisper to myself. She'll get well because we've made so many plans. She's teaching me to knit, to bake. Next Christmas we'll make fruitcake together.

I hear Belle murmuring to Olivia. I can't make out the words, but her tone is loving.

"Will you remember your promise?" Olivia asks, and she sounds like a small child. "Will you?"

Belle murmurs again.

Next door to me, Yolande sticks her head out her door. Her hair is tangled and she isn't wearing her glasses. She squints at me. "Is Olivia awake?" she whispers.

I nod. Yolande's eyes fill with tears and she shuts her door.

I tiptoe down the hall and rap on Grandmother's door. She opens it instantly, wide awake, pale in the pale morning light. "I heard," she says. "It's getting earlier every day."

Minette slips past me into Grandmother's room. "Yes," she says. "Belle didn't give her the shot until six-thirty yesterday."

Grandmother presses her fingertips to her mouth. Then she says, "And Belle was up with her at three this morning."

I go back to my room. Olivia had been in the hospital for weeks, but then a month ago she came home. I know why. *I really know*. But I've been telling myself every day that she's getting better, that I'll always have her, that she'll go on baking my birthday cakes and knitting sweaters for me. She is part of the mothering circle. If it breaks, what happens to me, to Colleen?

Ben is up. He stops outside Olivia's room to listen and then he whines. Someone, Belle probably, opens the door and lets Gip out. He's Olivia's dog, stiff and grumpy, but Ben adores him for some reason. Together they go downstairs. Grandmother goes with them to let them and the poodle, Markie, out. Markie sleeps downstairs on the sofa in Grandmother's office.

The day has begun. I dress and tame my wild curly hair. When I come out of my room, I can smell coffee. And I hear Belle's hearty laughter downstairs. "Look at that dog, Garnet," she says. "He's in the raspberry patch again."

Grandmother shouts at Ben. I pass Olivia's door and hear her humming. I was wrong — she's not worse. I worry sometimes about nothing. I run down to help Grandmother drag Ben out of the raspberries. What could go wrong on a day like this?

Breakfast is over before I remember the telephone call I got from my mother late last night.

"Gray," she said, "I thought you were going to call me when you'd made up your mind."

For a moment I couldn't remember what she meant. She didn't wait for me to sort out my thoughts.

"School," she said. "How can you decide anything if you don't come here to look?"

I have three more years of high school, and I don't want to move. But it would have been rude to tell my mother that, since she's acting as if she might want me around. So before I hung up last night, I agreed to go to San Francisco for a visit and let her show me the school she has in mind for me.

"You'll enjoy the trip," Grandmother said when I told her.

"But do you care if I move there?" I asked, hoping she'd say that she wouldn't allow such nonsense.

Grandmother, reading business papers in her little office off the kitchen, looked over her glasses. "Well,

I hope you don't. But you've got until September to think about it."

I wasn't satisfied with the answer, but she wouldn't decide for me, so I couldn't expect rescue from the trip to California.

After breakfast I call Colleen, listen to her whispered and hilarious account of the anniversary dinner, and then ask her if she's going to the flea market with Minette, Yolande, and me.

"How can you even ask?" she says. "I'll come over and help you load the truck. *He's* left for rounds at the hospital."

From the basement, Minette and I haul all the stuff she's collected during the week from garage and yard sales, incredible, wonderful, horrible articles that she'll resell at the flea market north of Seattle. Minette has a regular stall. We'll put out a folding table and arrange the junk as attractively as we can, and then sit in the shade of the truck and wait for customers. She doesn't need the money, she says. She needs the fun.

By eight-thirty, we're ready to leave. Grandmother, standing with hands on hips, studies the stuff in the truck. "You'll have a good day, Minette," she says. "I'm tempted to buy that magazine rack. But the lamp is so awful that it'll probably be the first to go."

Minette drives the truck. Yolande drives Colleen and me in Grandmother's car. Belle waves a languid good-bye from the porch, where she and Grandmother have their coffee on warm mornings. Ben is in the raspberries again — I can see his long tail waving from the depths of the bushes.

Colleen has brought something to sell at the flea market, a magenta satin teddy belonging to Fawn. "I found it in the dryer," she says as she takes it out to look at it again. "Isn't it terrible? Where does she find this stuff? Do they have a store that sells clothes exclusively to prostitutes?"

Yolande and I laugh. "Why am I getting the idea that Fawn doesn't know you have her tasteful undergarment?" I ask.

Colleen snickers. "She doesn't. I wanted to bring some of her jewelry, especially the lizard with rubies in it, but she's wearing everything today. She's going to the tennis club for lunch."

"She'll knock 'em dead," I say as we follow the truck onto the freeway. "Grandmother dropped her membership because the club was filling up with 'sweaty people.' She says that a long time ago hardly anybody actually played tennis and nobody perspired. She can't get used to modern life."

"I wish my father wasn't trying to," Colleen says. "Do you know that he's practically as old as your grandmother? He's fifty! He has fake hair, a fake tan, a girdle, and he's had his face lifted."

Yolande erupts into laughter. But Colleen is sober and angry.

"What does Fawn see in him?" she goes on. "Of course, what does he see in her? Last night she barfed up dinner and dessert both. She made so much noise puking up her food that everybody in the living room could hear. And her girlfriend did the same thing. Don't they realize we know what they're doing?"

"They're sure to charm everybody at the tennis club," I say, my eyes on the truck ahead of us. The ugly lamp has fallen over, and its shade is bouncing on the lawn chair Minette found in a ditch. We're close to the turnoff so we pull into the right lane.

"If Aaron asked you for a date, would you go?" Colleen asks suddenly, surprising me with the change of subject.

I look at her, then at the back of Yolande's head, wondering if she's heard. "He isn't going to ask me out," I whisper, but my heart is beating faster.

"He's cute," Colleen says. "Just think, if we went to his school instead of ours, you might have been dating him already."

"You'll probably date him before I do — if he ever looks at either of us."

"I'm saving myself for Doug Merriweather," Colleen says.

Doug Merriweather lives down the hill, close to Colleen's house. He's seventeen and he doesn't actually know either of us. He has a motorcycle and rides around without a shirt. We know who he is the way girls always know about guys like him, even bores like us. He has what Grandmother calls a reputation. Belle saw him roaring past once and referred to him as a cool dude. He reminded her of the fellow she'd been married to for six months, she said. The rest of us laughed at the idea of Belle ever being married to a cool dude, since she only dates an elderly dentist now.

"But you stay away from Doug," Belle had told Colleen. "Guys like that always leave you with insomnia."

Aaron doesn't qualify as a cool dude, thank goodness. I have enough insomnia.

Yolande parks the car at the end of the lot, and we hike back to where the flea market people are setting up shop. More than half of the stalls are already filled. Most of the vendors put their goods out on tables, but some simply dump theirs on the asphalt and then retire to their trucks or cars to eat snacks and drink out of bottles concealed in paper bags. These people are slightly sinister, and the rest of us keep away from them.

"Good morning," a fat lady with grizzled hair calls to us as we pass. She's arranging antique crystal on a table spread with a heavy linen cloth. A delicate vase contains sweet peas.

"Good morning, Mrs. Carmody," we say.

We nod to Mrs. McArthur and old Mr. Dixon and the elderly Carpathian twins who sell handmade baby clothes. A new vendor is setting up next to Minette, an unpleasant-looking woman who studies Minette's goods with greedy, resentful eyes.

Minette pats the lampshade back into shape and inquires about the contents of Colleen's paper bag. Colleen shows her the hideous teddy and Minette laughs. "Oh, it's awful," she exclaims. "We'll hang it from the lamp. It'll sell."

The woman next to us hungers for the teddy — I can see it in her little brown bean eyes. She's hanging dusty, faded garments on a wobbly rack. Perspiration already stains her shirt.

The flea market opens at ten, and a long line of hot and impatient people surges through the gates. Within five minutes, the teddy sells to a familiar-appearing young woman who looks as if she has her hair curled with jumper cables in the same salon where Fawn goes two or three times a week. She, also, is so thin that she's flat-chested and looks bow-legged in her skintight clothes.

"Aren't you Colleen?" she asks. "Fawn Clement's stepdaughter?"

Colleen nudges my ribs with her elbow. "Oh, do you know Fawn?" she says as she stuffs the teddy into the same crumpled bag she used to carry it here. She holds her hand out for the fifty cents that she's charging for it.

The skinny woman hands Colleen two quarters and reaches for the bag. "We work out at the same gym," she says. "I see Fawn nearly every day. Wait until I show her this darling teddy."

"She'll love it," Colleen predicts with a straight face.

When the woman teeters away on her spike heels, Colleen collapses against me, laughing.

"Fawn's going to kill you," I say.

"In a million years I couldn't have planned anything better than this," Colleen says.

I have to pat her on the back before she can breathe again properly, and even then she begins whinnying out her crazy laughter again and again for the next hour. Whenever we catch a glimpse of the teddy's new owner strolling in the aisles, we laugh. Finally we tell Minette and Yolande what Colleen's done.

"I ought to be furious that you tricked me into selling stolen goods in my stall," Minette says to Colleen, "but it's too funny."

Yolande, wiping tears from her eyes, promises us that she'll put the story in her next book. Colleen screams with laughter now.

"What's so funny?"

I look up, to see a tall, dark boy standing in front of us, smiling too confidently. He's wearing tennis whites and looks exactly like the sort of guy most mothers would want for their daughters.

"We're laughing at a private joke," I tell him.

"You work here?" he asks. "At a place like this?"

"Certainly," I say. "I get a commission on everything I sell." It isn't true — Colleen and I come along most Saturdays just for the fun of it.

"I hope you're a serious customer and not just a cheap flirt," I add. "I need the money." Colleen and I have learned how to make people feel guilty.

The boy looks around, appalled, and stumbles over his feet. "Oh," he says. I enjoy his anguish and watch him while he paws through our junk until he finds the magazine rack.

"You ought to buy that," I say seriously. "You could take it back to college and use it for your copies of GQ."

"Sure," he says. Colleen nudges me again. Yolande is looking away, biting her lips.

"That'll be twenty dollars," Minette says, her voice loud and brisk. "It's an antique, you know. Old. Very old."

The boy pulls out his wallet and extracts a twenty dollar bill. I almost feel sorry for him. But not quite. He's a snob and a jerk.

"I'll see you around some time," I say, doing my best to sound businesslike.

"Good clothes!" the woman in the next stall bawls suddenly, startling us. "Good clothes here." She isn't looking directly at the boy, but I can tell she recognizes a sucker when she sees one.

He flees, with the magazine rack banging against his long, tan legs. The four of us laugh helplessly, leaning against each other.

"I don't know what I'd do without you," Minette cries, fanning herself with an old plastic placemat, also for sale.

The sun blasts down on the asphalt. At noon, Colleen and I go to the snack bar and wait in line for hot dogs and soft drinks. A boy in soiled jeans smiles at Colleen until she turns her back. He's one of those who sell stuff off the ground, and he smells of beer.

Even in the flea market, people are divided into classes. Minette may sell junk but she's a Waverly, and no Waverly drinks out of a bottle hidden in a paper bag.

"Our drunks all used Waterford crystal and passed out on Aubusson carpets," Minette said once. She was referring to both her long-dead husband and Olivia's. They had been alcoholics.

The crowd grows larger. Half of Minette's treasures are gone. We'll leave when she decides that the day is too hot or the remaining goods won't sell fast enough to make the wait worthwhile.

"Go take a walk," she tells Colleen and me. "Yolande and I can handle things."

We stroll up one line of stalls and down another, gossiping with the vendors, trying on old clothes, and sorting through jewelry and books, looking for things to take home to amuse Olivia. We don't talk about her, though. Neither of us can bear it.

We go back to Minette's stall. She and Yolande are folding up the table because they've sold nearly everything. The sun is like molten brass now. The grumpy woman next to us still has most of the dusty clothes on her rack, and she is bawling, "Good clothes!" in a voice that can only frighten away customers.

After we pack the truck, Colleen decides to ride back with Minette to keep her company. She waves as Minette eases slowly out into the crowd, heading toward the exit. Then Yolande and I find the car at the far end of the lot and get in. It's an oven. We get out and stand beside it, waiting for the heat to dissipate. At last we head for home.

There are long, hot shadows in the yard when we arrive. Colleen is waiting on the porch with the dogs. We go in, calling out to Grandmother, but she doesn't answer. Yolande runs upstairs.

Colleen looks at me and I look at her. We hear soft muttering voices upstairs.

"Wait here," I tell Colleen, and I mount the stairs slowly.

". . . much longer," I hear Olivia say.

"No, darling, of course not," Grandmother says. "We promised you. It'll be anytime you say."

"Whatever you decide is what we'll do," Belle says.

I slip back downstairs. "Let's get something cold out of the refrigerator," I say.

"What's wrong?" Colleen asks.

I see myself in the hall mirror. I'm so pale that the gold freckles on my nose stand out. "Nothing's wrong," I say.

In the kitchen, I pour ice water into glasses for us and hand one to Colleen. My hand trembles.

"It's almost four," Colleen says. "Will we have tea?"

"We always have tea," I say. "Come out on the porch."

When the clocks strike four, we hear the tea cart rattle.

"Thank heaven," Colleen says. Then, suddenly, she laughs. "Do you suppose Fawn knows yet who has her teddy?"

"I guarantee that she won't keep you waiting when she finds out," I say. "Especially since you only charged fifty cents."

"My goodness!" I hear Grandmother exclaim. "Aaron's out there scraping the dollhouse windowsills in this awful heat."

I see him now, by the side of the dollhouse. "Aaron," I call, "tea's on." My spine prickles.

He looks up and I think he's smiling, but from this distance I can't be sure. He's shy, I tell myself. I can wait.

But all I do is wait, I think with sudden and suffocating dismay. My story has no end. I don't know why I'm here or what will happen to me when this endless summer burns itself out into autumn.

Why did my mother leave me here? Does she want me back?

I should have demanded answers before, but it's so easy to drift along in my grandmother's house, where the clocks have no hands, where the teatime stories are familiar and consoling.

For the first time in my life, I am embarrassed by my circumstances, and when Aaron runs up the porch steps, I turn my head away.

❧ Chapter 3 ❧

Sunday morning breakfast is served in the kitchen at nine. Yolande and Minette pass strawberry pancakes to Grandmother, Belle, and me. Olivia is asleep — finally. Belle says she probably won't wake until noon.

We share the Sunday paper and pretend that everything is fine. Belle drinks cup after cup of strong coffee. Her eyes are bloodshot and weary, but she laughs lustily when she reads aloud from the editorial page. Belle and Grandmother despise reporters, politicians, and lawyers, but not necessarily in that order, and so they always find something on the editorial page that causes them to roll their eyes up and shake their heads.

Colleen phones shortly after ten. "The world is coming to an end," she whispers. "Fawn found out about the teddy, and I'd be dead by now except that her brother was arrested last night for burglarizing the convent across from St. Pat's."

I didn't know that Fawn had a brother, but I'm pleased that he's in trouble. That will distract her father from the fifty-cent teddy, I tell her.

"Shall we still pick you up at eleven-thirty?" I ask. Colleen and I visit her mother every Sunday for lunch. Yolande drives us there and picks us up again.

"I told *him* that I really need to go to church today." Colleen's voice changes abruptly. "So if you and Yolande could pick me up at the usual time, I'd appreciate it, Gray."

Her father or Fawn has come into the room and she'll hang up now. But before she does, I say, "Does Fawn want her teddy back?"

" 'Bye now," Colleen says. She's trying not to laugh.

The sky is overcast and sullen, but Grandmother and Belle take their coffee out to the porch, accompanied by Ben and Markie. Minette attacks the dishes.

"Is Colleen seeing her mother today?" Minette asks.

"Sure." I pick up the last piece of bacon and nibble it.

"How's Lucy getting along?" Minette closes the dishwasher door and fills her cup with the last of the coffee.

"She wants to find a better apartment," I say.

Minette looks up, curious. "Lucy isn't expecting Colleen to move in with her, is she?"

I shake my head. "She knows better. *He'd* do something awful. He told Colleen that if she tries to see her mother, he'll have Lucy put into the asylum again."

Belle's come in to ask for a fresh pot of coffee. "Baloney," she says. "He'd have a hard time pulling off that stunt again. Lucy's been doing fine for years."

"He makes her crazy," I say. "When he found out that she gave Colleen a birthday present last year, he called Lucy a dozen times every night until she had her phone number changed."

Belle stares at me. "Why didn't you tell me that?"

"She didn't want anybody to know," I say. "Dr. Clement even tells everybody that Lucy's likely to try killing herself again. He says things like that in front of Colleen's friends."

Belle, her crippled hands fumbling with the coffee container, spills half of it on the floor. "Oh, damn, damn," she cries. "Just thinking about that man makes *me* crazy. Every time I see him, I want to step on him and squash him into turkey poop."

"Spoken like a true lady and physician," Minette says, laughing, and she pushes Belle away from the spilled coffee. "Let me clean it up."

"There's a nurse at the hospital who's looking for someone to share her house with her," Belle says as she sits down by the table. "She hates Kookie Clement. I'll tell her about Lucy. Maybe the two of them can get together. It's a nice house."

I go upstairs to dress. As I pass Olivia's door, I hear a meditation tape playing. Belle sets the stereo to rewind and play the tape over and over because it helps Olivia sleep. I peek in the room. Olivia is a lump under her quilt, barely breathing. Gip, curled at her feet, looks up at me and whines. I creep away, swallowing hard.

When I'm ready to leave, I discover that Aaron is here again, scraping the last of the dollhouse windowsills. When he sees me come out on the porch, he nods.

I'm a little early, so I walk over to him, wondering even as I do if I should be taking the initiative this way. Aaron watches me. My footsteps falter.

"How come you're working on Sunday?" I ask.

"Dad told me to," he says. "He had everything scheduled. He wants me to start painting soon."

"But you've got all summer," I say.

"It's going to take all summer to paint these buildings," Aaron says. "That little gazebo will be a real problem. Mrs. Templeton doesn't want the vines disturbed, so I'll have to reach behind them with a small brush to get the lattices."

I turn to look at the summer kitchen. "It's not a gazebo," I tell him, for lack of anything else to say. "It's a summer kitchen. It's got a fireplace with a stove-top to cook on, and water, and electricity. It's not just garden decoration."

He must think I'm crazy — I'm arguing about what to call the summer kitchen. I don't want to argue. I want to find something we can agree on and discuss, a reason for us to go somewhere else to talk. A common interest so he'll say, "Why don't we get together some evening?"

Instead, he says, "Okay, summer kitchen. Whatever." And he goes back to his scraping.

I get into Grandmother's car and Yolande drives us away. My face burns.

Colleen's waiting for us on her front porch. We've barely come to a stop when she yanks open the passenger door and flings herself inside.

"Please get going," she says. "They're having a no-holds-barred battle. Fawn's brother is here. He's actually named Lance — can you believe it? My father got a lawyer for him, but what good will a lawyer do? Lance broke into a *nunnery!* He says he thought it was a vacant building because it was so quiet. So my father says, 'What did you think you'd find in a vacant building, you little bastard?' and Lance says he was looking for a stray cat or dog to adopt."

"You're making this up," I say as the car turns onto the freeway. Colleen's mother lives in town.

"I am not making anything up!" Colleen says. "My father's so mad that he forgot to put on his hair this morning, and Lance didn't recognize him when he first got there. 'Fawn, you jerk,' Lance said. 'What's Money Bags going to think about you letting the old man in the droopy shorts hang around here?'

My father poured himself a drink, and it wasn't even nine o'clock yet."

Yolande and I are laughing, and a boy in the car next to us honks and waves. "Is Lance going to stay with you?" I ask.

"I guess," Colleen says. She stops laughing abruptly. "How awful. I hadn't given it much thought, but he really is going to be there, until his trial at least. Then I suppose he'll be in jail, unless this lawyer — his name is P. Q. Murphy — can get him off. But a *nunnery*, Gray. That was so stupid that he might just as well have broken into the police station."

My mind has recoiled at the name P. Q. Murphy. The women in my grandmother's house know that name. It figures in one of the chapters of my unfinished story.

"What's wrong?" Colleen asks. She is looking at me, curious, a little alarmed.

I shake my head to clear it. "Nothing," I say. My mouth is dry. P. Q. Murphy is the lawyer who defended the man who killed my father. Doesn't Colleen recognize the name? She's heard the story many times over the years. Yolande remembers the name — I can tell. She sits so straight and silent at the wheel.

She lets us off in front of a small brick apartment building. She'll spend the next hour and a half in her favorite downtown bookstore, looking at other writers' children's books.

Lucy is waiting for us. Every Sunday she fixes us lunch, a wonderful salad with hot rolls, and delicate, jam-filled pastries for dessert. She looks like Colleen, with soft, dark hair cut short around her heart-shaped face. But her hair is shot with white strands and there are lines around her eyes.

She hugs us both and leads us to the small table already set. "You look so tan," she says as she serves the salad.

"Saturdays at the flea market," Colleen says. "It's the hottest place in Washington State."

Colleen tells her mother everything that happened during the last week, including the incident with the hideous teddy and Lance's failed effort to launch a one-man crime wave against the sisters in the convent.

Lucy recognizes the lawyer's name immediately. "Oh, no," she says, looking at me. "Is that awful man still alive? I was sure someone would have murdered him by now."

Colleen looks from one of us to the other. "What am I missing?" she asks.

"Didn't you know that this Murphy is the lawyer who defended the man who ran over Gray's father? He's the one who made Norah sound like a rattle-brained hysteric while she was testifying."

"What?" Colleen asks, sounding panicked. "He's the one? I'll tell Fawn and my father. He should hire somebody else to defend Lance against the nuns."

I shake my head. "It doesn't matter," I say. Then,

suddenly, I begin laughing. I'm out of control, bent over my plate and howling. "Do you know how crazy all this sounds?"

Colleen and Lucy laugh, too. "It could have been worse," Lucy says. "What if Lance had been caught robbing the food bank or a shelter for the homeless?"

We are still laughing on our way home. A gentle summer rain is falling, and I wonder if Aaron will still be there when we arrive.

"I really will tell my father about that Murphy creep," Colleen says. "But he won't do anything. You know how much he hates your family. Your grandmother has this way of putting him down, and he's never sure if she means it or not."

"Trust me when I tell you she means it," I say, grinning.

"And Belle is rude to him whenever she sees him at the hospital," Colleen goes on. "It makes him so mad that she's this big famous consultant."

"Keep going," I say, snickering. "Get to the good part."

In the front seat, Yolande is laughing aloud, anticipating what comes next.

"Ha ha! Oh, help, I can't go on," Colleen groans. "I can never talk about what your mother did without coming unglued."

"Your father hates my mother," I began, "because . . ."

"Because she slammed his hand in the door when he came over to see if she was lonely and needed somebody after your father died." Colleen leans back against the seat and roars.

"You didn't quote him right," I say. "If you're going to tell teatime stories, you have to repeat everything correctly. Belle says your father told my mother that she probably needed her bed warmed up, and he'd be glad to give her some of his time, and then Mother said she had a hot water bottle that was better looking and slammed the door on his hand. And while he was yelling on the porch, Grandmother threw a pan of cold water on him and told him that's what her mother always did to her weird uncle Willie when he pestered her."

We try to get a grip on ourselves as we turn into Colleen's driveway, but we're still laughing when the car stops to let her out. A grubby guy with dirty hair is smoking on the porch. He raises his hand in greeting when Colleen climbs the steps.

"Pee-yu, Lance," Colleen drawls, fanning the air as she passes him. "What are you smoking?"

"Hey," Lance complains, "this is good stuff."

Colleen slams the door behind her, leaving Lance and me staring at each other through my open window. He smiles, showing small teeth like Fawn's, except his are green and hers are capped.

"Yuck," I say, and Yolande drives away. I look back and see him make a gesture that probably represents his best shot at elegant wishful thinking. He's in the right house.

At home, Aaron and Grandmother are conferring

on the porch. "Aaron's ready to paint," Grandmother tells me when I join them. "But it's raining."

"It might not last long," I say. I feel so awkward, with big hands and feet. Of all the boys I know, only Aaron makes me feel this way.

He watches me, sober and quiet, his eyes shadowed by his lashes.

"I hope you'll be around for dinner," Grandmother says to me. "Olivia's coming down."

She doesn't add that Olivia won't be coming down for many more dinners. She doesn't need to. "I'll be here, of course," I say.

I go inside. Ben slides in with me, woofing gently at me, talking Great Dane talk. He's worried. Olivia was always the one who fed the dogs twice a day, and now the rest of us do it.

"Didn't you get your food?" I ask him, as if he could answer.

"I fed the dogs," Belle shouts from the kitchen. "But I was late, and they didn't know what to make of it so they didn't eat." She limps down the hall, massaging her hands. "Should I fix them their dinner at the regular time or wait until later tonight?"

I shrug, looking at Ben for help. He makes soft mooing sounds to Belle, his forehead wrinkled.

"Lord, I hate this," Belle explodes. "Nothing goes right. Why can't I make things go right around here?"

Belle and I wrap our arms around each other, silent in our misery. Ben leans against me, mooing again.

"It's okay," I tell Belle. "Honestly. We're managing everything fine." But I'm a liar and Belle isn't deceived.

When the clocks announce teatime, Belle and Minette are in the dining room waiting. Yolande comes into the kitchen from the dollhouse, ink smudged on her chin. She pushes the tea cart for Grandmother.

"I saved the thickest cookies for you," Grandmother says. "Do you want lemonade?"

I nod and glance toward the window. I don't hear anything on the porch.

"Oh, he went home," Grandmother says, reading my mind.

Upstairs, the meditation tape continues playing. Gip comes down to the kitchen, yawning, drinks from the water pan, and climbs the stairs again.

"How was Lucy?" Minette calls from the dining room.

Standing in the doorway, I tell them about the visit, pacing my tale the way they do theirs so that there's a beginning, a middle, and an end. My beginning starts at Colleen's house, so that I can include the anecdote about Lance and the nuns. When I finish and everyone is laughing, I see Grandmother nod at me. She's pleased, I think, that I can tell a story properly.

Well, why not? I've been listening to master storytellers all my life. Perhaps I'll be invited to sit with the rest of them soon.

"P. Q. Murphy," Minette says, with a deep sigh. "Isn't it amazing that no one's murdered him yet?"

"That's what Lucy said," I say. We laugh again.

That P. Q. Murphy was responsible for my father's killer going free is an old wound, thickly scarred over. His name hurts us a little, but he is part of the story of this house and everyone in it.

"I wish he knew how much we laugh at him," Belle says. "There's nothing like a little humiliation to spoil a piss-ant's day."

Minette and Yolande help Olivia downstairs at six-thirty. She is wearing her best dress and the shawl I made for her after she taught me to crochet. They've fixed her hair and made up her face. She looks frighteningly ill.

"Oh, you look so beautiful," I tell her as I bend to kiss her after she's seated at the table.

She nods as if she believes me. Grandmother brings in Olivia's favorite food, baked salmon with mushrooms. The salad has an orange and almond dressing. Yolande pours wine for everybody but me. I have cold cider.

Olivia raises her glass, and I will myself to stay dry-eyed.

"To our mothers," she says, her voice quiet and strong. "All of them, clear back to Eve."

That night I have a good dream of women sitting in a circle in a meadow, telling stories. I wake to hear Belle's voice.

"No, go back to bed, Garnet," she tells Grandmother. "I'm handling it."

"But you must be exhausted," Grandmother says.

"She'll sleep now," Belle says. "She felt bad because she couldn't visit Rowena's grave once more."

"But it's in Oregon," Grandmother says. "Could we manage it?"

"Impossible," Belle says. "There's no time."

I sit up in the dark and clutch my pillow to my chest. No more time? So soon? The memories of all the winter afternoons when Olivia patiently taught me needlework, all the summer mornings she helped me bake cookies, rush past me like fleeing birds.

"When?" Grandmother asks.

I cover my ears so I can't hear Belle's answer, and when Grandmother looks in my door a moment later, I pretend I'm asleep.

My next dream is terrible. I see a dark figure whirling down a street ahead of me, beckoning, beckoning. I wake, gasping, paralyzed with fright.

In the thin dawn light, Ben raises his head and his dark, gentle eyes calm me. "Groo-oo?" he inquires.

"I'm okay," I say. I fall back asleep with my hand on his narrow brindle back.

❧ *Chapter 4* ❧

I wake late on Monday morning, hearing breakfast sounds downstairs. Outside my windows, weak sunlight falls on the lawns and gardens. Beyond the summer kitchen and the dollhouse, the woods lie still and silent. Below me, Ben and Markie investigate the invisible trails left by night visitors — raccoons and 'possums, perhaps even the mountain beaver who picks the bush beans.

Cornelius Ert arrives in his rattletrap truck, his monstrous lawnmower glowering in the back. Ben and Markie rush inside. They are terrified of the lawnmower.

I lean on my elbows to watch. Emaciated Cornelius is Grandmother's age, but he has none of her wit and charm. He wrestles the lawnmower from the back of the truck and skids it down a wooden ramp to the driveway.

Grandmother comes out. "For heaven's sake, Cornelius," she says. "I told you that you couldn't mow the lawns today."

"It's been a week," Cornelius says without looking at her. He searches through his pockets, finds a handkerchief, and blows his nose explosively. "I do my work on time, that's what."

"I appreciate it, but Olivia isn't well, and we're afraid that the noise will disturb her. I *told* you that." Grandmother intimidates everyone except Cornelius.

He removes his baseball cap and resettles it. "I'll be done in a couple hours. Then I'll clean out the patch of nettles in the orchard."

Grandmother has been after him to remove the nettles for weeks. No one can walk under the trees without being stung. She hesitates, then says, "All right, but don't come near the house. Just do the lower lawn."

Cornelius watches her go inside and then spits on the grass. Belle appears, using a cane to steady herself.

"Listen, you," Belle says, "that contraption of yours better be working right today. If it starts coughing and bothers Olivia, I'll fix you and your lawnmower both, and you won't like it."

She returns to the house and Cornelius spits again. But when he starts his mower, it is quieter than I've ever heard it. He's always liked Olivia.

I dress and leave my room. As I pass Olivia's doorway, I see that Gip is sleeping on her bed, tucked against her back. The tape is rewinding. Then the machine clicks and the music begins again. It's different. Someone bought Olivia a new tape.

Downstairs, Grandmother, Belle, and Yolande are dawdling over coffee. Minette, at the sink, looks up when I come in.

"Well, sleepyhead," she says to me.

"Did Olivia get much rest?" I ask.

Belle and Grandmother exchange a look I don't understand. "She had an easy night," Belle says. "What are your plans today?"

I fill a glass with juice and sit down at the table. "I thought I might hang around here."

"Is Colleen coming over?" Grandmother asks.

I shrug. "I don't know. I'll call her later."

"Call her now," Grandmother says. "It's nine. She'll be up. Ask her if she can help you and Yolande with the grocery shopping. We've got a list and it's big this time."

I stare at her. Minette does the shopping now, since Olivia got sick. Of course, nobody ever sends Yolande alone when she's in the middle of a book because she's too absent-minded, even if she has a list. "How come Minette's not going?" I ask.

"I have an awful headache," Minette says. Her face is averted and I can't see her expression.

Belle is looking at me. In her eyes, I see sorrow and pity and something else. She's begging me to go. She wants me out of the house. This must be the day.

"Oh," I say, as if someone had just punched me in the stomach. "But Olivia's going to the doctor this week," I blurt. "Maybe . . ."

Grandmother's look silences me. "Of course she's going," she says. "Why wouldn't she?"

I can't think. I try to swallow juice but it won't go down.

"Gray," Belle says sharply, dragging my attention back to her. "Will you look out to see if Aaron's here yet?"

Without speaking, I stumble out the kitchen door. Aaron is busy with buckets of paint near the dollhouse. In the distance, the lawnmower putts and burbles. A Steller's jay flaps down near Aaron and challenges him. Aaron looks up and laughs, then sees me and waves lazily.

I return to the kitchen to report on Aaron. Minette has laid out the grocery list and several twenty-dollar bills. "Give Colleen a call," she says, still not facing me directly. "You'll need all the help you can get. You know how Yolande is."

Obedient because I don't know what else to be, I march to the phone and call my friend. Fawn, the idiot child-bride of Dr. Clement, answers by chirping, "Dr. Clement's residence."

Tacky, I think. Grandmother says only pretentious people answer the phone with anything but hello. I ask for Colleen.

Fawn chirps, "She's in the bathroom. You wanna wait?"

While I wait, I wonder why no one ever told Fawn that she shouldn't offer that particular bit of information to telephone callers. Colleen comes at last, and says, "Did she tell you that I was in the bathroom? She always does that. She even says that if someone calls when my father's in the bathroom. But Lance is even worse. He says 'can' instead.''

I can't help but laugh. "It sounds as if your whole family spends all its time in the bathrooms.''

"I know," Colleen says. "It's some sort of deadly coincidence. No one calls here anymore unless at least one of the johns is occupied. Can't you just imagine what people think? I KNOW, I KNOW, JUST LEAVE ME ALONE!''

The last sentence was meant for Fawn, not me. I'd been hearing her whine in the background.

"Can you get out of the house?" I ask. "Yolande and I are doing the grocery shopping, and we have a list a mile long.''

"Pick me up as soon as you can," Colleen says. "My father grounded me but he's gone." She lowers her voice. "Can we go to the store where Doug works? He's on day shift now.''

"Sure, but don't expect to hang around there all day.''

"Why? Do you have plans with Aaron?" Colleen laughs.

Through the window, I can see Aaron painting the dollhouse. "No, I don't have plans with him." But I wish I did.

Minette is standing behind me. I wonder if she heard. Colleen tells me to hurry and hangs up.

"You girls should have lunch somewhere," Minette says.

"How can we if we have frozen stuff?" I've read the list.

Minette fumbles for an answer and finally finds one. "Leave that until later. I don't need the frozen things for lunch."

"You mean make two trips?" I don't know why I'm making this hard for her. But I am, deliberately.

Minette shrugs. "Well, I guess that was a stupid idea. Maybe you could bring the groceries home and then go out to lunch."

"Maybe," I say vaguely. Suddenly I throw myself at Minette, wrapping my arms around her neck. "Don't make me go," I whisper. "Oh, please, I can't stand it if you make me go."

She leans her head against mine. "Hush," she murmurs. "It's not what you think. Nothing's going to happen."

"Please don't lie to me."

"I won't," she whispers. "We plan to spend the morning together. Gossip about old times. It's for us old gals. You and Yolande would be bored."

I'm gripping her back so hard that I must be hurting her. I unclench my fingers. Relief pours through me. This isn't the day. They wouldn't sit around Olivia's room all morning drinking coffee and gossiping if she were dying now.

Grandmother gives me another list before I leave, a smaller one for the drugstore. "Just a few odds and ends," she says.

I read it. Nothing unusual. "Okay," I say. "We'll be back whenever we get here."

Aaron sees me leave and waves again. Cornelius has finished mowing and is working in the orchard. Yolande drives us away, concentrating on the road. Everything is fine.

Colleen is waiting on her porch again, but before she has a chance to get into the car, Fawn comes out on the porch. She's wearing neon pants and a tight shell. No one in this world looks less like a fawn. Her brown hair is streaked with orange, and her eyelashes droop with mascara. "How long are you going to be, Colleen?" she whines. "Who's going to help me fix lunch?"

"Lancie Boy," Colleen snaps. "Drag him out of bed and hose him off. If he's hungry, he can help you fix his swill."

Fawn minces inside and slams the door.

"Three more years," Colleen says. "Then I'm eighteen and out of here."

"Tell *him* you're moving in with us now," I say. "What's he going to do?"

"Make trouble for Mother and your grandmother," Colleen says. "He'll make trouble anyway. But he can't accuse anybody of corrupting a minor then."

"Corrupting a minor!" I say. "What's that supposed to mean?"

"It's what he threatened to accuse your grandmother of doing if I run away to your house," she says.

"That's dumb," I say, "but where your father's concerned, anything's possible."

We are still talking about her father when we pull into the parking lot at the store where Doug Merriweather works. We see him as soon as we go inside, working at one of the cash registers. "He really is cute," I whisper to Colleen.

Her face turns red. "He's gorgeous," she says.

We need two carts, and we push them up one aisle and down another, with Yolande trailing behind us, dawdling and reading labels on everything. Minette is getting enough food to last us a month, I suspect. Ten cans of tomato sauce? We all like pasta, but ten cans? And six boxes of rice.

"Are you expecting an army to move in?" Colleen asks.

My throat hurts. I can't answer for a moment, and then I say, "We're big eaters."

"And there are six of you," Colleen says. "I guess this isn't so much after all."

Six. Not after this week. Sometime this week we'll only be five. I know that. Maybe not today, as I'd thought, but soon. Olivia is drifting away from us. She wants to leave now. Last night was the last time she'll come down for dinner.

"I hate chocolate cake that comes from a mix," I say, full of sudden, scorching anger. "Olivia always made cake from scratch."

"How is she?" Colleen asks.

"Not bad," I lie, sorry I mentioned her.

At last we're done. Both carts are piled high when we get in the line at Doug's register. He's stuck with a woman who waited until he told her what she owed before she showed him her coupons and started searching through her purse for her checkbook. Ordinarily I would move to another line, but I know that Colleen would be devastated.

By the time we're second in line, Doug has noticed us. He smiles at Colleen frequently, even though he doesn't know her name. But he must recognize her. She's been strolling past his house for weeks, and dropping in here to buy six-packs of Coke or potato chips or bags of cookies.

Our turn comes at last. "Paper or plastic," Doug says to me, but he's looking at Colleen again.

"Paper bags, please," I say. "We recycle."

"Good," he says, smiling at Colleen.

Even though he's flirting with her, he's still careful about ringing up the right prices. I'm in a picky mood, so I'm watching him closely. I'd like to find something wrong with him, and stupidity will do just fine. But in the end he's done it all right, so I don't have anything to complain about. While I count out the money, he asks Colleen where she lives.

"I see you around," he says to her. I have to work hard not to laugh out loud. See her around? How can he miss her?

She tells him where she lives — and her name.

He looks at me when I hand him the money. "You live in the big house on Crest. I've seen you in the yard with a Great Dane."

I nod. He's not interested in me, but I don't want Colleen to think she has any competition.

He calls a bag boy over to help us, and smiles at the next customer. Colleen is nearly in shock as we go out to the car.

"Isn't he darling?" she asks. The bag boy laughs.

"He's all right," I say. The shopping took over an hour. We forgot to go to the drugstore first, and now we don't dare stop because of the frozen food.

At home, Colleen and Yolande help me carry the food inside. The phone rings the moment we reach the kitchen.

It's Dr. Clement, calling to find out if Colleen's here. "Tell her to get home right now and help her stepmother," he yells.

I deliver the message. Colleen hesitates for a moment, and then tells me that she'd better go. It's good politics, she says. No one's forgiven her for the teddy. After she leaves, I become aware of the quiet. No one is downstairs, not even Yolande.

They're in Olivia's room.

I climb the stairs, my sneakers silent on the carpet. Now I hear soft voices. I look in Olivia's doorway. She's propped up in bed, and she smiles when she sees me. Relief washes over me, cool and clean.

"All done shopping?" Minette asks.

I nod. "But we forgot to go to the drugstore first," I tell Grandmother. "We've got a whole sack of frozen stuff."

"Put it away, will you?" Grandmother asks. "I'll come down later and put the other things away.

Meanwhile, I'm afraid we've forgotten about lunch and Aaron must be starved. Will you make something and take it out to him?"

"Sure." I lean over Olivia, taking one of her hands. "How are you feeling today?"

Her eyelids are heavy and she blinks drowsily. "I'm fine, darling," she says.

She's wearing her favorite bed jacket. The bed's been made up with old, pressed linen sheets, the ones edged with wide lace and embroidered with my great-grandmother's initials. I've never seen them used before. They scent the room with lavender. The white curtains at the windows stir in a quiet breeze that carries the smell of freshly mown lawn.

Yolande is holding a book. She's going to read aloud to Olivia again. Belle, sitting on the small sofa near the wall, watches me, her dark eyes compelling me to walk softly, carefully, through my part in this play.

I pat Olivia's hand. It's so cool, too cool.

"Run along," Grandmother says. "Poor Aaron, he's starved."

I go down to the kitchen. I'll think of Aaron's lunch and nothing else. Belle's eyes are still watching me from inside my mind. Keep going, she wills me. Keep going and don't look back. This isn't the time to look back. Later we'll do that.

Aaron will eat anything we fix for him. I make him one tomato sandwich and another of ham and cheese. I take a cold soft drink from the refrigerator.

Cornelius is getting into his truck as I step outside. "Tell your grandmother that I took care of the nettles," he says.

"Okay," I say, and I keep walking.

"See you next week," he says to my back.

I nod but don't stop. Aaron sees me and sits down on the bench beside the dollhouse door. "Lunch," he says. "Good."

He offers me one of the sandwiches, but I shake my head. I don't know what to do with myself. I can't go back inside. But I can't stand out here watching him eat, either.

"Sit down," he says. I sit.

"Do you like science fiction movies?" he asks.

At first I don't understand him. "What?" I ask. "What?"

He grins. "I asked you if you like science fiction movies. If you do, maybe you'd like to see one with me tonight."

"I don't think so."

"Oh." He clears his throat. I've embarrassed him.

There's nothing in the world I'd rather do than go to a science fiction movie with Aaron. But I can't tonight. The world is grinding to a halt. Things are happening that I don't understand, and I need time to think about them.

"Maybe we can do it some other time," I tell him.

"Sure," he says.

I see my bedroom curtains stir. Minette is looking out at me. She doesn't want me here tonight. Belle appears next to Minette. Even from here I can read her eyes.

"Well, I guess I could go," I tell Aaron. I barely recognize my own voice. A sigh rises from deep inside me.

"Would you like to have dinner first?" he asks. "Pizza?"

"Sure," I say.

He reaches over and takes my hand, just as I took Olivia's. "Your grandmother said that Mrs. Thorpe's feeling fine," he says.

I nod. "Yes, fine."

He squeezes my hand and then lets it go. I'd like him to hug me, but he doesn't know that, and so we sit side by side. Ben comes out to raid the raspberries, and a crow scolds him.

I'm getting my wish and going out with Aaron but I'm too numb to appreciate it.

❧ *Chapter 5* ❧

Yolande, nervous because of the afternoon traffic, drives me to the drugstore for Grandmother's shopping, to the dry cleaners for Belle's blazer, and to the library to return Minette's books. Grandmother and Minette are busy in the kitchen. Belle dozes in Olivia's room.

Between errands, Grandmother sends me upstairs with Olivia's tea. Belle asks for sherry, which surprises me because she says that it tastes bad. I bring it up right away and find her bending over Olivia, whispering, whispering. Olivia is smiling.

Belle's telling her another of her simply awful dirty jokes, I think, grinning. Things can't be so bad. I'm making mountains out of molehills again. I feel better when Yolande drives me to the yarn store to match Minette's embroidery thread. She's too nervous to read, she says.

At five, Aaron leaves, after telling me that he'll be back for me in an hour. It's really happening. I've been trying to report this to Colleen on the phone, but whenever I'm home, she isn't. I try once more before running upstairs to shower. Child-bride answers and whines that Colleen still isn't back from grocery shopping, they can't start dinner until she returns, and the doctor is on his way home and there's going to be hell to pay.

Yolande is in the bathroom at our end of the hall, so I shower in the other one, hurrying and smiling. When I bolt out into the hall, I collide with Grandmother, who was coming out of her room. Something falls from her hand.

"Sorry, Grandmother," I say, and I laugh like an idiot. You'd think I'd never gone to a movie before.

I bend down to pick up what she dropped — a pill bottle. But she bends, too, and snatches it out of my hand.

For a moment both of us stare at it. The bottle is full of small, red capsules. She folds her fingers around it and holds it down at her side.

"I'm so clumsy," she says. But her face is stiff with shock. Why? Why?

"Are you sick, Grandmother?" I ask. I can't remember the last time I saw her taking medicine.

"Sick?" she repeats. "I'm a little tired, Gray, that's all. Shouldn't you be getting ready to leave?"

My watch is in my room and Grandmother doesn't wear one. Is it late? *Why does she have those pills?* How sick is she?

"Grandmother," I begin.

"Go on," she says, giving me a little shove with her free hand. "You don't want to keep Aaron waiting."

I hurry off, but farther down the hall I look back. She's watching me. I go into my bedroom and close the door.

I listen. I hear Belle's door close, not Grandmother's.

I'm still standing there thinking about this when someone knocks on my door, scaring me. "If you don't get downstairs," Belle says, "I'm going out with that boy instead. He looks like a sweetheart to me, and if you don't want him, I do."

"Okay, okay," I say. Did Grandmother send her to my door, or is Belle so relaxed this afternoon that she can tease me?

In fifteen minutes I'm downstairs, and before I have a chance to worry about whether or not Aaron's coming, he drives up in a blue car. When he gets out, I scarcely recognize him. He's wearing a beautiful white sweater, and he looks so glamorous that for a moment I think about going back upstairs to change into something better than my last year's cotton dress.

Grandmother is bending over the banister. "See you later. Have a good time," she calls down, committing me to going as I am.

"Kiss him for me!" Belle yells from the upper hall.

I flee out the door, hoping that Aaron hasn't heard her. He's walking toward the porch.

"You look pretty," he says, "but then, you always do."

Ben makes his mooing sound from the porch swing where he isn't supposed to sleep, but he doesn't trouble himself getting up.

Aaron opens the passenger door of the car and grins down at me. Suddenly I'm so delighted by possibilities that I almost don't want to look up at the second floor windows where Olivia sleeps.

But I do. Have a good evening, I think. I'll see you when I get home, if you're awake. Otherwise, in the morning I'll tell you all about my date.

Now that I've reassured myself, I can lean back and return Aaron's smiles.

He takes me to a pizza place I've never been in before. During dinner, he tells me about his school and how glad he is to be starting his junior year in the fall. He's more talkative than I thought he'd be. I hear about his father, how he quit practicing law because he hated it and his fellow lawyers, how he set himself up in the house-painting business.

"What does your mother do?" I ask.

"She's a nurse. She works for a doctor named Roderick." Aaron is looking down at his plate and I can't read his expression. Does he know Dr. Roderick is Olivia's oncologist?

"I know Dr. Roderick," I say. "He takes care of Olivia."

Aaron looks up, surprised. "I'm sorry," he blurts.

I feel blood pounding in my head. "Maybe she's

one of those people who'll get over cancer," I say. "Having it doesn't mean you're going to die!"

"I know, I know," he says hastily. "Sorry. Of course she's going to be cured. Why else would she be home from the hospital?"

I look away from him. He's got to know what a dumb question that was. There's another reason people leave the hospital. They come home to sleep away what's left of their lives.

There's an awkward silence to endure. Finally, Aaron says, "I can't help but hear your grandmother and the others talk when they're having tea. Your mother lives in San Francisco?"

I nod.

"Have you ever lived there?" he asks.

"No. I went there to visit once, but — well, it didn't work out so I came back early." I help myself to another slice of pizza and don't look at him.

I was supposed to spend two weeks with Mother the summer I was eleven, but she was gone all day and I hated being left alone in her spooky house. When I told her that, I'd hoped that she'd say she'd take a few days off and spend them with me — that had been the original plan, after all. But instead, she called Grandmother and then drove me to the airport for the next plane. "We can try this again when you're older," she said. Now I'm older. So we're going to try again.

Aaron pulls his salad closer. "I know your father is dead," he says. "I heard the women in your house talking, saying that he'd been killed when you were a baby."

I nod. "A man robbed a store and my father saw him running out the door. The robber got into a car and ran over him."

Aaron winces. "That's terrible. I hope he went to prison for the rest of his life."

I sip my soft drink and look at the wall behind Aaron. "Actually he went free. Later, just a few years ago, he died in prison, but he was there for some other reason."

"You mean he didn't get punished because of your father?"

"That's right," I say.

"Doesn't it make you mad?" Aaron asks.

I look up at him. He's upset. At me? Because I'm not angry about the man who killed my father?

"I've known about what happened all my life," I say. "I guess I was angry, but mostly I was sorry that I didn't have a father. When Grandmother told me the man died, I was glad. But, well . . ."

He's stopped eating. "How about your mother?" he asks.

"She never talks about it," I say. "Not ever. If I try to bring it up, she refuses to listen. She hates the way Grandmother and the others talk about things. She calls it 'rehashing the past.' But I like it."

Aaron nods. "I do, too. I like listening." He blushes suddenly. "I didn't mean that the way it sounds. It's not as if I eavesdrop, but I can't help hearing."

"I know." I laugh. "You're sitting on the porch and they're inside the dining room window. You'd have to be deaf not to hear them. Cornelius knows everything about Yolande's divorce, and when her ex-husband showed up at the house wanting to make trouble for her, Cornelius hit him with a rake and scared him off."

Aaron laughs helplessly, finally sliding down in his seat and gasping. "I can see it," he says when he gets his breath back. "Old Corny running after some guy with the rake."

I giggle. "It *was* funny. Grandmother called the police and accused Yolande's husband of trespassing, and told them that if it hadn't been for Cornelius, a whole houseful of helpless women would have been at the mercy of a wife-beater. It was great. Cornelius practically got a medal. Yolande's ex-husband needed stitches in his scalp."

"Good," Aaron says.

We take longer eating than we should, and when we get to the theater, the movie has started. I tell Aaron I don't care, so we go in anyway.

The movie is a long one, and when we come out it's past ten o'clock. Aaron drives slowly once we're off the freeway, and I'm glad. I want to savor this time.

We turn in the driveway much too soon. Aaron stops the car by the porch and opens the passenger door for me.

"Thank you for coming," he says. "You're lots of fun."

"So are you," I tell him.

"Maybe we can do this again." He looks as if he means it.

"Yes, maybe," I say. "Yes."

I watch him leave and let myself inside.

Belle is standing in the hall with her back to me, talking on the phone. "Let me speak to Dr. Roderick," she says. "Tell him this is Dr. Russell."

Time stops. I can't move. Olivia is worse. I shouldn't have gone to the movie.

Belle looks back over her shoulder at me and starts to say something, but instead listens to someone speaking on the phone. "Yes, it's me," she says. "I'm calling about Olivia. It's over. Yes, in her sleep. No, you don't need to. Yes, if you would. Yes, I'll tell Garnet and the others."

I hear every single word. I'm not spared anything. When Belle hangs up, she turns to me.

"Olivia's gone," she says. "I'm sorry, baby. I'm so awfully sorry, because I know how much she meant to you."

"I shouldn't have gone out," I say.

"It wouldn't have changed anything," she says. She reaches for me and hugs me. "It was time."

"I should have been here."

"No, no, baby. It was better this way."

Something's choking me. I push Belle away. "You knew it would be tonight, didn't you? That's why you and Grandmother wanted me to leave."

Belle fishes a tissue out of her bathrobe pocket and

wipes her eyes. Tears fall, one after another. She doesn't try to stop them, she just cries. "You can never tell about these cases, Gray. But we all knew it was coming."

I need to hear the whole story. I already know the beginning and the middle. But Belle is keeping the end from me. "You and Grandmother, even Minette and Yolande, knew that it would be some time today. I'm part of the family. I should have been here."

Belle blows her nose. "Your turn's coming. You'll stand a death watch, too. But now you must leave that sort of thing to the women."

I've begun crying and I can't stop, either.

"Do you want to see her?" Belle asks.

"Is Grandmother with her?"

Belle shakes her head. "No. She and the others said their good-byes, and now they're resting. If you like, you can go upstairs. The men will be here for her pretty soon."

"Who?" I ask. "Who's coming?"

Belle hugs me again. "Some people are coming to take her away, Gray. But if you want to see her, you'd better go now."

I climb the stairs. Olivia's door is open and the lamp on her dresser is burning. The rest of the room is shadowed. Cool night air blows in. Gip is gone and I wonder where he is.

Olivia's blanket is pulled to her chin. She seems to be smiling. I touch her hair, and then I leave.

Grandmother's door opens. "Ah, Gray," she says. Her eyelids are swollen. Gip tries to run out the door but she grabs him.

"I'll go down and see if I can help Belle," I say, and I reach out and touch Grandmother's shoulder. "We'll talk tomorrow. Try to rest, Grandmother."

Her door clicks shut and Gip whimpers. I return to the kitchen and find Belle drinking coffee.

"Go out to the dollhouse and sit with Yolande," she says. "She ran out there after . . . Take her a cup of coffee. It'll help you to keep busy."

I fill a mug for Yolande and carry it across the lawn. Clouds drift slowly past the moon. Deep in the woods, an owl calls.

The dollhouse door is open. Inside, Yolande is sitting at her keyboard and her computer screen is scrolling as she reads back what she's written. She's crying as she works.

"Coffee, Yolande," I say.

She reaches for the mug. "I saw you come home," she says. "Belle told you?"

"Yes."

"It went faster than I thought it would."

I don't want to stay and talk, even though I can tell Yolande wishes I would. I can't give her the help she needs tonight, because my own hurt is too great. "I'd better go back," I say.

But when I leave, I see headlights coming up the driveway.

No, no. I can't watch what comes next.

I head for the woods, to the place where the owl mourns. Ben appears from somewhere and walks beside me, leaning against me and moaning. Behind us, I hear Markie barking, men talking.

I sit down on a log and cry. I look up and my eyes are filled with the silver glitter of tears and moonlight.

A long time after I hear the men leave, I go back to the house and enter through the kitchen door. The light's on, but the room is empty. The counter is cluttered with the remains of a quick meal, bread crusts and orange peels. Automatically I open the door under the sink and begin scraping plates into the garbage pail.

Then I stop.

There's a crushed hypodermic in the pail. Belle always crushes hypodermics with pliers after she uses them, so that no one can take them from the dump and use them. I slam the door shut.

They had promised Olivia that they would do what she wanted when the time came. I always knew what they meant.

When I go upstairs, Belle is waiting for me in my room. She looks terrible.

"What's wrong?" I cry. What next? I'm thinking.

"Oh, it's that goddam dog," Belle weeps.

"Which one? What's happened?" I can't seem to breathe.

"Gip wanted back in Olivia's room," Belle says, "and after they took her away, I thought, well, why not? Poor mutt. Poor damn dog. And then I went in there a few minutes ago, just to check on him."

I'm afraid of what's coming. I sit down on the bed beside her, squeezing my fingers together.

"He was lying on her pillow," she says. "The poor beast. He died right there on her pillow."

This is unbearable. I wind my arms around Belle and we both weep silently, rocking each other.

Downstairs, the blind clock in the hall announces that it is one o'clock in the morning — after the day Olivia died. We have already plunged into the future and left her behind.

Chapter 6

Tuesday is a day of hushed phone conversations and murmuring visitors in the living room. Grandmother, erect, every hair in place, presides over our small meals. Yolande, tangled hair streaming down her back, fled to the dollhouse after breakfast. We hear the chatter of her printer through the open door.

Around noon, Cornelius and Aaron arrive in the same truck. They consult with Belle on the porch, and then Aaron comes in, climbs the stairs, and descends again with Gip. He, or someone, has wrapped the dog in a flowered sheet.

"Where are you taking him?" I ask Aaron. My voice is hoarse. I know I look horrible.

But Aaron's smile is gentle and accepting. "Dr. Russell arranged for a pet cemetery to cremate him. Corny and I are taking him out there. And tomorrow we'll bring back . . . we'll bring . . ."

"I know," I say.

"I'm sure sorry about everything."

He carries the small bundle to his truck. Cornelius takes the bundle and holds it in his lap as Aaron drives away.

Colleen comes during lunch, red-eyed and upset. She refuses a sandwich but accepts a glass of water.

We sit on the porch swing together. Ben and Markie wouldn't come out with us, but instead lie at the foot of the stairs waiting for Gip. This makes Colleen cry again.

"Why does God let the wrong people die?" she demands. "Fawn is the one who should be dead. Fawn and her rotten brother. Oh, I hate him so much I could kill him myself! Why aren't they on their way to be cremated like Olivia and Gip?"

She's ranting, unusual for her. "What's wrong?" I ask.

"I can't bother you with it now," she says. "I came to help you, and I don't want to end up telling you the latest adventures at the House of Horrors."

"Go on, tell me. Maybe it'll make me laugh."

She shakes her head. "It's not making *me* laugh."

"You have a funny way of telling things. Go on. I need to hear all the latest news."

She still won't smile. "Don't blame me if you're sorry you asked. Yesterday I rode my bike to the store and came back late. Hey, Doug asked me for a date! Well, sort of. I'll tell you about that later. Anyway, I got home, and there was my father, Fawn, and that drooling idiot of a brother. Boy, were they mad! I had four pork chops and a package of frozen vegetables, you see. They carried on like I'd deliberately stayed away with the medicine that could have saved somebody's life. Oh, sorry! I didn't mean to remind you of Olivia."

But I think of Grandmother's pills and the hypodermic in the garbage. Colleen doesn't know about them. She thinks that I'm remembering all the times people tried to cure Olivia.

"It's okay," I say. "What happened next?"

"*He* and Fawn went out to dinner, leaving me alone with Lance. Now you won't believe this, but it's true. Honest. I was in the kitchen fixing myself something — because I absolutely refuse to cook for that slob — and he came up behind me and . . ." She collapses suddenly with hoots of laughter.

Ben, hearing the racket, sticks his head out the door, stares, and then withdraws it.

"I thought you couldn't laugh," I say. "Tell me the rest."

"Wait," she gasps. "Wait till I can breathe. Oh, ah. You won't believe it."

"Not if you don't tell me what it is I'm supposed to believe."

She wipes her eyes on her sleeve. "He came up behind me and stood really close, sort of pressing against me, and he grabbed me. He — you won't believe this — he actually *groped* me, or at least he tried to. He stuck his hand up under my shirt."

"Oh, yuck!" I cry. "That's disgusting! What did you do?"

She snickers. "I was holding a fork, so I poked it in his wrist as hard as I could. I remembered how your mother treated my father that time."

I laugh. "Good for you. Did you make him bleed?"

"Not much," she says. "But did he ever scream! He locked himself in the bathroom, bellowing like a lunatic."

"So what did you do?" I ask, fascinated.

"Heck, I washed off the fork with hot water and soap and got the dill pickle out of the jar for my sandwich," Colleen says.

I'm impressed. I don't think I could bear living in the same house with Lance. She probably should have used something sharper.

"What did your father say?"

She's grinning. "When he got home, Lance had already called this lawyer, P. Q. Murphy, because he wanted to put me in juvenile detention for assault. So my father called the lawyer and said that if he wanted money to keep Lance out of jail for robbing the nuns, he'd better stay out of a family fight. The lawyer wasn't going to do anything, anyway. He told my father that Lance is a moron, and he's lucky that I didn't call the police because *he* was trying to assault *me*."

"It's like a soap opera," I say. "What happens now?"

Colleen scowls and folds her arms. "I'm supposed to stay home and behave myself, whatever that means, and Lance has to keep away from me or he gets thrown out."

I put down the plate that holds my lunch. I'm not hungry. Ben sticks his head out the screen door and moans anxiously. "You can have it," I say, and I hold out the sandwich. He gulps it down, then looks around the yard. He's still expecting to be bullied out of things by Gip.

I have a lump in my throat so big that I can't talk. Colleen reaches for my hand and squeezes it. "When I called last night, your grandmother said that you'd gone to a movie with Aaron, and that you'd tried to call me about it."

I nod. "Olivia died while I was gone."

"Maybe that's better. You'd have felt even worse if you'd been here."

"I don't think so."

She sighs. "Well, at least she died in her sleep." She snorts, suddenly angry. "My stupid father says that maybe Belle put Olivia out of her misery. He says he wouldn't put anything past a woman doctor because they think with their hormones. But you know how jealous he is of Belle. He can't stand it that she's invited to speak at conventions and on television. He especially can't stand it when she's on TV. But he watches anyway, and his face gets so red that I expect him to have a stroke."

I hear her but I don't hear her. Everything she says

registers on my brain, but I seem to be stuck at the words, "Belle put Olivia out of her misery."

What do I do now? What do I say? Is there danger here?

I sip my soft drink and say, "There isn't going to be a funeral. Did Grandmother tell you? We're scattering Olivia's ashes — and Gip's, too — on Puget Sound."

"Oh, I love that idea," Colleen says.

Cornelius' truck rattles up then. "Tell Miz Templeton to get out here on the porch," he says. He's gruff and scowling.

I get Grandmother. Minette and Belle follow us. While we watch, Cornelius pulls a huge wooden planter filled with flowers from the back of the truck. His strength astonishes me. He totters to the porch and places the planter next to the steps. "This is to remember Miz Thorpe. I'll bring new flowers for it every spring." He honks his nose on his handkerchief.

Grandmother's crying, but she's smiling, too. "Thank you, Cornelius. Those are all her favorite flowers. Thank you for remembering."

"That's not all," he grumbles. He stomps back to the truck and takes out a small terra-cotta planter containing a peach-colored miniature rose. "This is for the girl," he says, and he hands it to me. "But it's not from me," he hastens to add. "I don't give flowers to young girls, no sir."

I'm afraid someone is going to laugh at what he's

said, but no one does, not even Belle. There's a folded piece of paper stuck among the rose leaves. I put down the planter and read the note.

"For Grayling. I miss them, too. Aaron."

I put the note in my pocket and move the planter to the broad porch railing. "Is this a good place for it?" I ask Cornelius.

He ignores the difficulty I had speaking. "No, it's not. Move it over there, where it can get some sun or you'll kill that little piece of silliness before the summer's over."

Apparently he doesn't trust me to carry out the task, for he climbs the steps and carries the planter a few feet away and puts it down with a thud. "There," he says. "But those little bits of nothing usually don't make it through the winter."

And with that dismal prediction, he leaves us. After his truck disappears, we all look at each other.

"Trust Cornelius to brighten our lives," Grandmother says.

She, along with Belle and Minette, go back inside. Colleen and I sit down on the swing again.

"I bet Aaron is crazy about you," she says. "That rose is beautiful."

"He's just being nice," I say, but I hope that he's crazy about me. Fat chance, I think, just in case nothing ever comes of us. I don't want to embarrass myself by expecting too much.

"He's probably nicer than Doug. I mean, Aaron doesn't roar around on a motorcycle, showing off

73

his muscles and flirting with all the girls he sees. But Doug is so darling. And he asked me if I'd go riding with him some evening after he gets off work."

"On his motorcycle?" I ask. Her father will kill her.

"No," she says. "I told him that would scare me. He's got a car, too. He says we'll go for a drive and get something to eat."

"That doesn't sound like a real date," I say. "Colleen, are you sure you want to do this?"

She looks straight at me. "Think how mad my father will be."

We rock and the swing creaks. "Getting involved with some guy just for revenge doesn't sound like the best idea you've ever had. You don't really like him, do you?"

"He's good-looking and funny." She holds up one hand to silence me. "I know. He's not my type. But who is? What boy ever came back to see me after the first time? My father always manages to spoil everything. I figure he'll have to work overtime to spoil anything with a boy like Doug."

I hear the phone ringing inside. Grandmother answers.

"I hope you don't expect too much from Doug," I tell Colleen. "He looks interesting but not too reliable."

"Yeah," Colleen says. I can't read her tone of voice.

Grandmother comes to the door. "Your mother wants to talk to you, Gray," she says.

I go in and pick up the phone. Mother tells me she's sorry about Olivia, but after all, we knew it was coming.

"Yes," I say.

"I forgot to ask about the funeral," she says.

"There won't be one," I say. "We're going to scatter her ashes over the Sound."

"Oh, for pity's sake," Mother says, exasperated. "Whose idea was that? Can't somebody else do it? I'm sure Mother could hire someone to take care of that."

"We want to do it," I say.

"It's morbid," Mother says. "I'm not sure you should be involved with something like that."

"I'll be fine," I say. "Are you coming to Seattle?"

"I can't," she says. "I'm so busy that I hardly have a chance to eat. Gray, I think this would be a good time for you to come to San Francisco and look at the school."

She just contradicted herself. If she doesn't have time to eat, how can she have time for me? But I don't point this out.

"So I went ahead and made reservations for you," she goes on. "I'll pick you up at the airport Friday morning around ten-thirty."

"Friday?" I ask, astonished. "So soon?"

"Well, yes," she says. "Don't think that I'll insist you live with me. But it wouldn't hurt you to con-

75

sider getting out into the real world now that you're nearly fifteen."

She's taking it for granted that I'm moving to San Francisco, I think. "I don't know," I say, deliberately vague.

"We'll talk it all over when you get here. I have to go, so tell everybody hello. Oh, yes, and tell them I'm sorry about Olivia. I'd send flowers, but under the circumstances, where would I send them?"

Where indeed? I think as we hang up. When I go back to the porch, I say, "I'm going to San Francisco on Friday. Mother wants me to live there."

Colleen looks surprised. "Do you want to?"

I shrug. "I don't think so. I'd hate being alone in a strange place."

"You'd have your mother," Colleen says.

"That's the same thing as being alone. I'd rather stay here."

Colleen looks around. "So would I. I can't wait to move in here when I'm eighteen."

I think about the vacant room on the second floor, but I don't say anything. Colleen wouldn't want to stay in Olivia's bedroom.

Colleen goes home when she's certain that Fawn is home from shopping. "That way I won't have to be alone with Lance. Fawn wants to buy a new teddy, and I told her to get a matching one for me. She said, 'Are you being snotty?' and I said, 'Who, me? Certainly not. We'd look like Tweedledum and Tweedledee, and then we can be best friends.' "

"I can see why she's mad at you," I say.

"She didn't know who Tweedledum and Tweedledee were. She thinks they're on TV." Colleen runs down the steps and waves. "See you tomorrow."

I stay on the swing. The sky is pale blue, almost gray. I take out Aaron's note and read it over and over. Olivia would have loved seeing the rose and the note.

After the drizzle starts, Aaron arrives.

"You can't paint now," I say when he climbs the porch steps.

"I know," he says. "I came to help you catch the rain."

"It's not coming down hard enough," I say.

Then I notice that Belle is watching us from the doorway.

"It's almost teatime," she calls. "Do you want tea or lemonade?"

"Lemonade," I say. "Okay, Aaron?"

He nods, and then sits across from me in one of the chairs for the first time.

Grandmother hands lemonade through the curtains. "Cookies?"

"Please," I say.

"Just look how I burned the bottoms of those cookies," I hear Minette complain. "I never could bake anything worth eating."

"They're fine," Yolande says.

"Olivia always burned the fruitcake," Grandmother says. "It never tasted bad, but Olivia would have a fit."

"She made good chocolate cake," Belle says. "Yum. That cherry filling."

Olivia has become a part of teatime in a new way. My mother should be here with us, helping to tell the stories of the women in this house.

"Oh, my, it seems so strange without Olivia," Minette says with a deep, hard sob.

"My God," Belle weeps.

"We'll be all right," Grandmother says. She's crying, too.

I don't realize that I'm crying until Aaron moves from his chair to the swing and slips his arm around me.

"Sorry," he whispers in my hair. "Sorry, Grayling."

Chapter 7

I'm surviving Wednesday by taking it five minutes at a time. On this bright blue-and-gold day, rain should be falling. The whole world should be weeping for our dead.

"Maybe you could take Aaron's lunch out to him," Minette says. "He insists that he's not hungry, but he must be." She looks at me curiously. "Would you like to eat with him?"

"I don't think so," I say.

Minette goes into the kitchen and comes back with a tray holding enough food for two. She pushes the tray at me and smiles. "You eat with Aaron."

I feel too self-conscious to enjoy the idea. Remembering my endless weeping the afternoon before, I think that Aaron's probably sick of me. But when I carry out the food, he stops painting and smiles at me as if nothing had happened.

As if nothing was happening between us.

Aaron, as a kind friend, brushes dust off the bench with a wad of paper towels and invites me to sit. He sits on the grass in front of me, and while he eats, he talks about Ben.

"He's been picking green apples all morning," Aaron says. "He takes a bite out of each one and spits it out."

"He thinks he's a vegetarian," I say. My face is stiff. It hurts when I talk.

Aaron takes a deep swallow of his Coke. "Your grandmother says you're going to San Francisco Friday to see your mother."

"Right."

"That'll be a nice break for you."

No, it won't. Why she wants me there I can't imagine. She'll be too busy to go anywhere with me — just as she was the other time I went there — and I'll spend endless hours sitting in her living room looking out the windows at her garden. Endless boring hours.

"San Francisco is a great place to visit," Aaron says. "We — my family — went there a couple of years ago. You can take a sightseeing bus or just walk. Or take the trolley. It's fun."

I put my sandwich down. I can't eat. "I was there once before but I didn't see anything except the road between the airport and my mother's house," I say, and the bitterness in my voice surprises me.

His expression is so sympathetic that I'm embarrassed. "Hey, do the town on your own," he says.

"But if you're like me, you'll be glad to come back here."

I don't say anything.

Neither does Aaron for a long time. Then he blurts, "You won't stay there, will you?"

I look up at him, meeting his frank, caring gaze. My heart beats thickly. He does like me. He really does.

I swallow hard so I won't burst into tears again. "No, I won't stay."

Suddenly I'm so uneasy that I begin babbling about the woods. "Did you know that if you follow the path back here, you'll find a creek?" I ask him.

"With stepping stones and an old statue of . . ." He stops and looks away.

"Of two people kissing," I finish. Both of us are embarrassed. "Grandmother's father fixed up the little glade with the statue and the stone bench."

"I didn't see a bench," he says.

I can't help but laugh. "You were looking at the statue," I say. "The bench is behind it, facing the water."

"Nice," he says.

I don't say anything more, but I wonder what he's thinking. And I'm embarrassed about what I'm thinking.

He goes back to painting — the dollhouse is almost finished. I return the tray to the kitchen. The clocks cry out the time.

Grandmother and Belle leave the house on errands. Minette is cleaning upstairs. Yolande calls her editor in New York, murmurs a few words and hangs up, calls her best friend and weeps.

"I can't write anything that makes sense," she says into the phone. "The computer lost half a chapter, but it wasn't any good anyway. I won't make my deadline."

Upstairs, Markie sits in front of Olivia's closed door.

What if someone discovers a cure for cancer today?

I feel like stone, barely able to crawl into my bedroom.

The day passes, creeping along like ice forming on a pond. In the evening, while the sky is still gloriously blue, we leave.

Minette, Yolande, and I ride with Grandmother. Dr. Roderick, Olivia's doctor and Belle's good friend, takes Belle in his car. They follow us to the dock in Edmonds, where we board the ferry as foot passengers.

Belle holds a paper bag with something in it. Dr. Roderick is carrying a shopping bag from one of Seattle's department stores. The large bag seems nearly empty.

Grandmother has a plastic jug that contains cold champagne, and a package of paper cups.

Minette carries two gardenias.

Yolande has only herself, and she clutches herself tightly because bits of her are shattering.

I hold a handful of tiny paper twists, each bearing a message for Olivia and Gip.

"If there are people on the rear deck, I'll lose my mind right here and now," Belle says.

"No, you won't," Dr. Roderick grumbles.

He is short and thick, with short, thick fingers, and a head of frizzy black hair. He scowls at us to keep us from crying. I've never liked him as much as I do now.

The ferry churns away from the dock, heading west, and we walk to our appointed places. The scarlet sun has dropped down to the rim of the Olympic mountains. Suddenly the western sky turns to wild flames, all gold and rose streaked with gushes of orange.

Dr. Roderick rests his shopping bag on the broad railing. Below us, the water seems to stream back toward shore, trailing froth. A cold wind chills me and I zip my thin jacket.

Three strangers join us at the railing, looking behind the ferry toward land. Belle moans. Dr. Roderick, holding the shopping bag handles with a white-knuckled fist, clutches her shoulders with his free arm. The people stare and move on.

"Oh," Grandmother says with a gasp.

Yolande is weeping now.

"Here, here," Dr. Roderick says to her, his voice sharp.

Yolande swallows her tears.

"I did what she wanted," Belle says suddenly. She buries her face in Dr. Roderick's shoulder.

He grips her tighter. "You were wonderful, dear

girl," he says. "Wonderful and brave and magnificent. Hold up your head."

My throat is paralyzed. I can't speak or swallow.

The sky over us is on fire. The ferry plows toward the line of black mountains across wild gold water.

"Now, Belle," Dr. Roderick says. "Now is the time."

Belle leans forward suddenly and tips over the small bag she's been carrying. A thin stream of ashes flies behind us and disappears into the fire and water and darkness. Good-bye, Gip.

I hear paper tearing. My head jerks around. Dr. Roderick holds the shopping bag in one hand and a small pocket knife in the other. He is slitting the bottom of the bag and the ashes of the body that contained our Olivia stream back to join Gip's.

Soon the fire is gone from the sky and water. Gentle dark blue twilight covers us. The waves glimmer with silver streaks. Ahead of us on shore, pinpoints of light shine.

Grandmother pours champagne and directs Yolande to serve us. We face the back of the ferry and raise our cups. Then, without speaking, Minette drops the gardenias in the water and I scatter the paper twists to the wind.

Safe passage.

Good-bye, good-bye.

We drink our champagne and Grandmother collects the cups and carries them to the trash bin. Then we go inside, find seats as far from the door as we can, and wait for the ferry to dock and then take us back to our own shore.

An ancient man approaches us, immaculately dressed in a neat suit and white shirt. He bows to Grandmother, and then to each of us. "So sorry for your loss," he says over and over. His hands are trembling. "So very sorry, friends. So sorry."

He leaves us amazed. We had not known we had an audience.

Dr. Roderick's eyes fill with tears.

"Garnet," Minette says, "do you remember the time you and Olivia and I took this ferry to the church picnic and that red-haired sailor flirted with Olivia?"

Grandmother smiles and clears her throat. "Of course I do. She wore a white shirt with green buttons. I remember it as if it were yesterday."

And so they tell Olivia stories, even Yolande, who ends up smiling. I join in, finally, telling about the time Olivia hid my burned cookies in the bottom of the garbage can so no one else would know what a mess I'd made.

Later, when we are home, and everyone else is busy in the kitchen making raspberry jam, I walk into the woods, to the creek where the lovers stand. I sit down and listen to the water splash over the stones. Behind me deep in the woods, the owl calls, its voice barely audible tonight. Moonlight filters through the trees. I smell damp earth and moss and crushed mint.

"Hello, Grayling? You out here? It's me, Aaron."

He calls me in a gentle voice, not wanting to frighten me, I suppose.

"I'm sitting on the bench," I say, knowing my voice will carry.

He sits beside me. "Dr. Russell told me you were here. How are you?"

"I'm all right," I say.

"I was worried," he says. "I phoned, and Dr. Russell asked me over to keep you company. She worries about you, too."

"Too much," I say. I'm thinking about the night Olivia died, when Belle urged me to go out, knowing what was going to happen. And I'm embarrassed that Belle has arranged this meeting.

I lift my head, stunned by a new thought. Did Belle arrange my date with Aaron?

The idea sickens me. I withdraw inside myself and slam all my mental doors shut against this boy.

He senses it. "What's wrong?"

"Nothing," I say, sullen now, wishing he'd leave. I want the night to myself.

He reads my mind. "I wanted to see you," he says.

"Sure," I say. "Just like you thought up the whole idea of taking me to a movie the other night."

He is silent so I know I'm right. I bite my lip so hard that the pain brings tears to my eyes.

Then he says, "I'd wanted to ask you to go somewhere with me for a long time, but I didn't know how to do it. I was sure you wouldn't go, until Dr. Russell said she thought you might."

"Wonderful," I say. I'm bitter and angry at everyone.

"It's hard for me to ask a girl for a date," he blurts.

"It's easier if somebody arranges it all for you," I say. "I mean, that's better than no date at all, right?"

"Yes," he says. "No, that's not true! I didn't want to take out anybody else."

"It's time for you to go home now," I say.

"No," he says, stubborn and cranky. "Not until we get this straightened out."

"It's straightened out already," I say.

Silence. "I really like you," he says.

You feel sorry for me, I think. Aloud, I say nothing. The night is spoiled. The lovers are liars.

"Yesterday, when you let me put my arm around you . . ." he begins.

"A mistake," I say. "I felt bad about Olivia."

Silence. "I wish you'd let me do it again."

What am I supposed to say? That I'd like it, too? That I need somebody I like a lot to hug me tonight? That I'm tired of waiting for life to happen? For something exciting to happen?

I turn to look at him.

He bends his head and kisses me, the kiss so quick and light that it's over before it registers on me.

We stare at each other in the silver night.

He takes my hand, looks down at it, strokes it gently, measures my fingers against his.

"Grayling," he says.

Behind us, the old lovers kiss forever. We kiss just

once more, and then Aaron walks me home, holding my hand the whole way.

I should be glad. But deep inside me I am so hurt. Belle arranged the movie date. Then it wasn't real. And maybe this isn't real, either.

❧ Chapter 8 ❧

On Thursday we try to pick up where we left off, but nothing is that easy. The day starts wrong and gets worse. Belle is ill, her joints so swollen that she can barely walk. Grandmother quarrels with someone on the phone, her voice cold and quiet. She seldom goes to the office where her buildings and other real estate holdings are managed, but now she must because somebody has failed her. Minette drives her there to keep her company. Yolande stays in bed until noon.

Aaron is painting the house, working on a scaffold. Ben moans at him from the yard, his forehead wrinkled with worry.

Colleen phones and I remind her that I'm leaving for California Friday morning. "Let's go out to lunch," I say. "I'll meet you at the bus stop closest to your house."

"*He* said yesterday that I can't go anywhere until the end of time," Colleen says, angry and almost shouting. "He lets Lance use one of the cars! Can you believe it? He lets a crook use a car but he won't let me leave the house. But I'll go anyway."

"Okay. Are you sure you can manage it?"

Colleen sighs. "Sure. Child-bride went to the tennis club for the day, so there's nobody to tattle on me. Lance wouldn't dare. If he does, I'll tell my father that he tried to rape me." She's shouting, so I know that Lance is listening.

"I don't know how you can stand to be in the same house with him," I say. "Look, get ready and meet me right away. We can eat and then walk around the Pike Place Market. I'll get something for my mother."

There's a short, expressive silence. Then Colleen says, "Since when are you anxious to please your mother?"

I'm startled. Since when? I never gave much thought to this remote, strange woman who lives a thousand miles away. Sometimes I wondered how she found it so easy to abandon me. Yes, that's the right word. Abandon.

That's a serious, almost violent action. What drove her to it? What's the reason she's kept secret from us?

"Gray? Are you still there?" Colleen asks.

"Oh. Sorry," I say. "My mind was wandering. I'm not trying to please Mother. Whatever gave you that idea? I guess Grandmother's rule is engraved on my brain. Always bring a gift for the hostess. You know how Grandmother is."

"Yes," Colleen breathes, sounding ecstatic. "Your house is so — I don't know — *orderly*. Everybody knows exactly what to do and what to expect."

Ha, I think. You'd be surprised what goes on around here that people wouldn't expect.

The hypodermic needle in the trash. And Belle's inconsolable grief, almost like a death itself.

How do I feel about that? I don't know. Yes, I do! Olivia was so sick. Her pain was so terrible. She wanted to fall asleep and not wake up. I knew that. I'd known that for weeks.

"What's wrong?" Colleen sounds alarmed.

"I don't know." I try not to sigh, but the sigh consumes me. "I can't seem to get going again."

"Don't think about Olivia," Colleen says. "Just think about having lunch and getting your mother something silly from the market. One of those pottery slugs, maybe."

"Oh, ugh!" I cry. My mother would loathe a pottery slug painted to look real.

"I was joking," Colleen says. "I'll see you right away."

When I hang up, I climb the stairs to my room to get my purse. Across the hall Belle's door is open, and she's sitting in her soft chair with her feet propped up.

"How are you feeling?" I ask from her doorway.

She smiles. "I'll live, darn it. That's what everybody who has arthritis says." She laughs, but her laughter isn't full and hearty. "Is that Aaron I hear moving around outside the house?"

"He's painting up high, under the roof," I say. "Do you mind if I go out to lunch with Colleen? Will you be okay?"

"Garnet will be back soon," Belle says. She laughs again, a sharp bark. "I feel sorry for her manager. She'll chew him out, blind him with her dirty looks, and be back here in time to fix sandwiches for that darling boy you're in love with."

My fists clench by my sides. "I wish you hadn't asked Aaron to take me to the movie," I say. I'd like to cry because I feel so bad, but I don't want to upset Belle. I only want her to understand that she must stop planning a romance for me. The story of Aaron and me would end up just another teatime anecdote, with the pain blunted by the constant retelling. Poor Gray — when she was almost fifteen she fell in love with someone who didn't love her back. The end.

Belle is embarrassed. "He wanted to take you out," she says, her voice rough and defensive. "I wouldn't do anything to hurt you, baby. He was too shy to ask you, so I helped things along, that's all."

"Please don't do it again," I say, and then to soften my words, I tell her that I'll bring up the morning newspaper for her.

Pain breeds pain. We are all injured because Olivia is gone. Now I trample over Belle, who meant to do the best thing for me but instead set me up for even more pain.

Colleen waits at the bus stop. "Where are we going to eat?"

I name our favorite restaurant at the market. The bus comes and we find seats in the back.

"How long will you be in San Francisco?" Colleen asks. "You said a few days, but what does a few days mean? I don't think I can hold up very long without you."

"Not more than a week," I say, but a part of me suddenly wants to stay longer. Even if I'm left alone in that house. I don't want to see Aaron for a while. I don't want to remember last night, either. I don't want to think about Olivia and Gip.

Colleen sighs. "Without you around, I'll have a hard time getting out of the house," she says. "I might not be able to see Doug or my mother."

"Sorry," I tell her. I'm truly sorry about her mother, but not about Doug.

"So what's new with you and Aaron?" she asks. "Has he asked you for another date?"

I shake my head and tell her Belle's part in my brief romance.

"Hmm." Colleen isn't too pleased about that. "Well, at least you did go out with him. Who knows? Maybe he'll ask you for another date all on his own. I bet he will. He'll miss you while you're gone."

I hope so. I hope he misses me so much that he can't sleep. The moon will be full while I'm away. Will he look up at it and think of the creek, the stone kiss, and the flesh-and-blood kiss?

Colleen and I eat and then tramp through the Pike

Place Market, admiring the vegetables and early summer fruit, dawdling over the crafts stalls, poking through the antique stores. At last I select a pound of wonderful fudge for my mother and a small spray of dried wildflowers woven into a picture frame.

"Are you going to give your mother a picture of you?" Colleen asks.

"No, I thought I'd give her one of Cornelius," I say.

Actually, I'll fill the frame with an old snapshot of all the women in my grandmother's house, including Olivia. Mother might like that. She doesn't stay away because she hates us — if she hated us she wouldn't bombard us with gifts and letters (they don't say much but they *are* letters) and irregular phone calls (they say even less than the letters).

For years I've accepted her absence with only the mildest curiosity. Now I'm anxious and angry about it. Why did she leave me to grow up with the storytellers?

Would I have enjoyed growing up in her house?

No. Actually, I don't like my mother very much. It isn't possible to like someone who is always running ahead of you and calling back frantic messages. *This is best for you. My life is so hectic that you'd be miserable here. I'm never home.*

"You're thinking about Olivia again, aren't you?" Colleen asks, interrupting my brooding.

"No," I say. But now I remember with pain as sharp as a razor that Olivia is gone, scattered in the wind and fire and water.

"I hope your grandmother doesn't expect me to take Olivia's room when I finally move in," Colleen says. We're walking back to the bus stop, squinting in a gritty wind.

"No, of course not," I say. "She'll fix up one of the rooms on the third floor."

Olivia's room, shades drawn forever, smelling faintly of lavender and delicate old linen sheets. Her empty chair in the dining room. How long does it take to forget about these things? The circle has been broken. What will happen to us?

"Is Minette going to the flea market Saturday?" Colleen asks as we board the bus.

"I asked her and she said absolutely yes. Her friends will want to hear about things. And going will make her feel better."

The bus edges out into the traffic and heads for the freeway. Colleen fans herself with an empty paper bag she found on the floor. We talk about school clothes and sharing a locker again. But we will make our own school lunches because Olivia is gone.

When we get home, Grandmother and Minette are sitting on the porch. Colleen and I sit with them. We can hear Yolande's printer chattering.

And Aaron is whistling overhead in an absent-minded way.

"How's Belle?" I ask.

Minette sighs. "She's asleep, I hope. She insisted on coming down for lunch, but she was on crutches. It makes me sick to see her suffer like that."

"Where's Ben?" I ask.

"Asleep in Belle's room," Grandmother says. "He's mournful, too. He misses Gip. Markie's under my desk chewing up my slippers. I should have scolded him, but he's upset about everything." She bends close to me and brushes back my bangs. "Are you all right? You look pale."

"I'm fine, Grandmother."

Inside the house, the hall clock bongs three times and the dining room clock echoes.

"I think I'll fix tea early," Grandmother says suddenly. "This day is dragging on and on. Early tea, early dinner, and early to bed. After all, we've got to get Gray to the airport by eight tomorrow morning."

"Eight-thirty will be soon enough," Minette says. "Yes, Garnet, let's have our tea now."

"Gray, ask Aaron what he wants, will you?" Grandmother disappears inside the cool house.

Colleen nudges me and grins. I get up reluctantly and step off the porch. High up, Aaron leans over the edge of the scaffold, his brush busy on the gingerbread work under the edge of the roof.

"Aaron, we're having tea early," I call out. "Do you want lemonade or tea or what?"

He looks down at me and dazzles me with his smile. "I'll have what you're having, Grayling," he says.

He never calls me Gray. Always Grayling. It sounds formal and inexpressibly sweet in his voice. Graaayling. The drawl softens the hard vowel.

Colleen is scarlet from suppressed laughter. Even Minette is grinning. "Graaayling," she whispers. "He's in love."

I shake my head angrily and go inside to help Grandmother.

It's barely three-thirty when she wheels the tea cart into the dining room. A breeze billows the curtains. The silver shines.

I go upstairs to help Belle down. She hobbles, swearing and scowling. "I'm too big for you to help," she says. "You should have called in your sweetie to help me. He looks strong enough."

I don't argue. She wants to have her little joke. Oh, Belle, I do love you so very much.

Colleen and I drink lemonade while we sit on the porch swing. Aaron, silent, almost smiling, drinks his on the steps. He is turned sideways, watching me from under his lashes while I try not to watch him.

Inside the dining room, Grandmother says, "I buzzed Yolande on the intercom but she didn't buzz back, so I guess she doesn't want tea today."

Minette sighs. "I hope she isn't spoiling for another one of her bad spells."

Belle sighs, too, lustily. "It's too bad all this caught her in the middle of a book. If she doesn't perk up by the time Gray's back, let's take her in for a session with Dr. Feel-good."

Grandmother laughs. "Belle, shame on you. Dr. Cook gave her so much help before that I don't know what would have happened without him."

Colleen pokes me with her elbow and raises her eyebrows. "A psychiatrist?" she whispers. I nod.

"Yolande would have felt just as good if Corny had bashed out her ex-husband's brains instead of only damaging him slightly." Belle's laughter rings out this time, full of life and loving.

Aaron laughs, too, a deep chuckle that he tries to stifle.

Belle's head pops through the curtains. "Yes, laugh, you young scamps," she roars at us. "But sometimes the only thing a person needs is revenge, and to hell with all the head-shrinking."

The three of us on the porch shout out our laughter then, until an outraged jay shouts back at us.

Inside, Minette says, "Doesn't that remind you of the time Olivia poured a sack of cement in her husband's car and wet it down with the hose?"

"Well, he was almost her ex-husband then," Grandmother says.

"He deserved it," Belle grumbles. "I heard that he'd been running around with that woman who worked in the bar and he had seven children with her without being married. They helped keep an adoption agency in business for years. If Rowena had lived, she would have needed to search in Europe for a husband because she was related to so many youngsters in this country."

Aaron buries his head in his arms. His shoulders rock.

Colleen collapses against me, giggling.

Teatime.

📍 Chapter 9 📍

I'm in the living room trying to concentrate on early evening television, but thoughts of Aaron interrupt me. And thoughts of the woods, where the water splashes on the stepping stones, where the air is scented with the wild mint crushed under our feet — where the stone lovers kiss. I hate myself for daydreaming, and I stomp out to the kitchen for company.

Everyone is sitting around the table playing cards.

"Hey, you, with good-looking boy chasing after you," Belle says to me. "Maybe you and I'd better have another long talk about the birds and the bees."

"Belle, for mercy's sake," Minette says. "She's only a child."

"Don't you remember Laura McGinnis from high school?" Grandmother says. "What was she — fourteen? fifteen? Somebody should have talked to *her*."

"Tell us about this Laura McGinnis," Belle demands. "She sounds like a naughty girl. I love hearing stories about naughty girls because then I don't feel so guilty about some of the things I did." Her laughter rings out so infectiously that everyone else laughs, too.

Grandmother and Minette tell Belle, Yolande, and me about the infamous Laura. The story has a beginning, a middle, and an end, of course. At least it has in this group of storytellers. I can't help but wonder if Laura, wherever she is, has learned their trick of taking the poison out of history.

We're all in bed by ten-thirty. My bag is packed. Tomorrow I'll sleep in my mother's house in San Francisco.

But I can't rest. When the downstairs clocks announce midnight, I creep out of the house, Ben at my side, and make my way through the woods to the creek where the stone lovers stand in the moonlight.

Someday, I think. Someday I'll come back here with someone who really cares about me, someone Belle didn't coax into spending time with me.

A night creature rustles through the brush on the other side of the creek. Ben stiffens and sniffs the air suspiciously.

My imagination flickers with dark and dangerous figures and I'm afraid. I grab Ben's collar and we run back to the house with moon shadows chasing us.

My slippers smell of mint.

*

At ten-thirty in the morning, my plane touches down in San Francisco. Mother waits at the gate, dressed in white, her hair streaked blond.

She chatters at me all the way to her house. We must leave the car in a garage she's rented two blocks away because her house isn't on a street, it's on steps called a hillclimb. In daylight, the hillclimb is beautiful, leading up between small, delightful front gardens. At night it terrifies me. I remember, while climbing it now, that the last time I was here I sat at my window at night watching the dancing shadows cast by the trees. If there were a place in this city where my nightmares might come true, it would be here, on these steps at night.

"I've had the second bedroom upstairs redecorated for you," Mother says as we turn in her gate.

"It looked fine before," I say. I don't want to be obligated to move here by new paint on the bedroom walls.

She unlocks the black iron grille that protects her porch from intruders. All of the windows in the house are covered with ornamental grilles. I remember from before that when we go inside, she will touch several buttons on a keypad in the hall to turn off the burglar alarm. My mother lives in a fortress. She must. Her house is filled with beautiful things, and it suddenly occurs to me that she is filled with fear, secreted under layers of sophistication as thick as enamel.

There's nothing alive inside her house. All the

plants are artificial. And she has no pets. There's nothing here that could ever need her attention.

We go up to the redecorated bedroom. It's pretty. The closet has compartments and shelves in it, with so much room that my few belongings look silly there when I put them away.

Mother is fussing with the curtains. "Do you like these? I remembered that you thought peach was a pretty color."

She really wants me to live here. "They're fine," I say.

"I should go back to the office today, but I thought we might have lunch somewhere instead and then I'll show you the school and anything else you want to see."

I shrug. "Sure."

"Well, what would you *like* to see?" she asks. She sounds hurt. "I know you didn't do any sightseeing last time. Things didn't work out for us. But you're older now, and you can be on your own sometimes. Girls your age like to be independent."

In one short speech she's moved from this visit to a future time when I'll be living here. She's taking for granted that I'll want to finish high school here. Why? Why now?

I need to ask but I'm afraid to embarrass her. Maybe I can figure it out by myself.

When we leave again we don't take the car out of the garage, but instead walk a few blocks and take the trolley downtown. After lunch she shows me her office in the company my father's father started. Several people are working, even though it's lunchtime, and they rush at Mother and ask her questions while she walks through the rooms. Her voice changes when she answers. She's brisk and a little sarcastic. Boss.

She still wears her wedding ring, although my father has been dead for nearly fifteen years.

A problem arises. Someone who should have done one thing did something else. Mother asks a young woman to find me a place to sit and a magazine to read.

I look out the window at the building across the street. After an hour, I find her and tell her I want to leave.

"I can get home by myself," I say.

"I'll call a taxi for you," she says.

She doesn't say that she'll be with me in a minute. She doesn't say she's sorry she's tied up and can't take me sightseeing. She gives me a handful of money, the keys to the house, and tells me the numbers to punch into the alarm keypad in the hall. They are the date, month, and year of my birth.

For some reason, learning that she's used the numbers for my birthday in her burglar alarm system makes me so grateful that I could cry.

And then my mother runs out of time and asks the young woman who gave me the magazine to call the taxi and keep me company on the street until it comes. And tell me about the city.

"Good-bye," I say to my mother.

" 'Bye, darling," she says, but she's already turned away and is pointing to a line on a page that a young man holds out to her.

As I leave the office, she calls after me, "I'll only spend a couple of hours here tomorrow. We'll have all of Sunday together."

"Thank you," I say.

I can't go back to that house and stay there all afternoon by myself. The taxi driver stops when I tell him to, a few blocks from my mother's office. I pay him and watch him drive away.

Overhead, the sky is bright blue. The sidewalk is crowded with an assortment of people that would cause Colleen to laugh aloud. A man in leather pants strides by. His beard is braided with strands of beads. A beautiful, elderly Asian woman passes, murmuring to herself. Two girls, twins, weave through the crowd, chattering in a foreign language. A tall boy with curly red hair stares down at me and grins, showing braces. He wears an earring. An old man waves a sign announcing the end of the world, and he shouts unintelligible words mixed with bizarre curses after me.

I go inside a shop that sells postcards and buy some to send home. I get a map, too. When I step back outside, I know how to find my way to Fisherman's Wharf.

I pass a hotel and the doorman glances at me. A lady with diamond earrings bends and slips into a long, white car. Her little dog barks and snaps at someone inside.

Near the wharf an ugly man in a pirate costume struts about with large, screaming parrots clinging to his shoulders and arms. I stare. He shouts that I must pay him a dollar to look at him. He smells so bad that I wouldn't stand there if he paid *me* the dollar.

When I've seen enough, I try to go back the way I came, but I've lost my way. A thick fog oozes in, so swiftly that I'm alarmed. On a street of shabby houses and apartment buildings, I unfold the map.

And I hear enchanting laughter from behind me.

❧ *Chapter 10* ❧

A young man stands behind me, legs apart, hands on hips. He is — astonishing! His black hair is close-cut and curly, and his skin is ivory, flawless, smooth as satin. His eyes glow golden through lashes as long as a girl's. He's dressed all in black — a running outfit under a long coat. He's no older than Aaron and yet he is *older* — older, somehow, than even Grandmother.

He smiles, showing perfect teeth, and cocks his head to one side. "Well, well, little girl tourist," he says. "You looking for somebody — or something? Me, Dancer, I find you anybody or anything. You name your pleasure and I fix you up. Yes!" And he laughs his wonderful laugh again.

I can't help smiling, especially when I see that he's wearing ballet shoes. "I think I'm lost," I say, and I hold out the map.

He shakes his head and leaps back a small step. "Dancer don't need no map, little girl tourist. Where you going? What you want to find when you get there?"

Suddenly I come to my senses. I shouldn't tell this strange boy that I need to find my way to Mother's. Danger flickers around him like sparks.

"I want to see Coit Tower," I say. It's at the top of the hillclimb. If I find that, I can find Mother's house.

He laughs again. "You sure that's all you want, little girl tourist?" he says. "Who you with? Mama and Papa bring you here to the big city and you get lost? Where you staying? What hotel?"

I shake my head. "I'm staying with . . . friends." I hesitated too long before "friends," and now he knows I'm lying. "I want to see Coit Tower," I repeat. "Do you know the way?"

"It's a long way to walk," he says. "Without company, that is." He flaps the sides of his open coat. "I got company for you. Name your pleasure."

He opens one side of his coat and before I'm sure of what I see, he hugs it to his chest. I had a glimpse of watches, many of them. I draw back and shake my head, turning away.

He leaps lightly around me and flips open the other side of his coat. Gold chains dangle there, dozens of them, necklaces and bracelets. He jiggles his coat and the chains click together. I can't pull my gaze away from the glitter.

"Aha!" he cries, and his laughter, golden as the chains, makes me smile again. "Now Dancer know what the child like — pretty little useless things!" He steps closer on his narrow, elegant feet. "You point to what you want, sweet girl, and I make you the best price in town."

"I don't think so," I say, but I'm laughing aloud.

He cocks his head again, staring without blinking into my eyes. "You not sure, though, little girl tourist. You think, maybe this wild dancer got what I want but he ask too much. We bargain, okay? How much money you got?"

I shake my head. "No, I don't want a chain. I want to know how to get to the Tower."

Something frightening clicks on behind his golden eyes. "Dancer, he not a travel agent," he says, the warmth gone out of his voice. He pirouettes, arms trailing as if the air were heavy, his long ivory fingers prettier than mine.

Abruptly he stops, facing me, too close now. "What you *really* want, little girl?" he says. "In all this ugly world, what you truly want? Me, Dancer, I get it for you. There's nothing I can't find, nothing I won't sell. Name it and it yours. For a price."

I back away, now more frightened than I've ever been. I can't even speak, but only shake my head.

I turn and walk rapidly toward the next corner. I pass a girl leaning against a pole, watching, smiling, her expression malicious. She wears spike heels, shorts, and a purple sweater.

"Hey, little girl tourist, you Goldilocks," the Dancer calls, "you be careful of the bears." His laughter rings out like bells.

When I'm a safe distance away, I look back. The girl watches cars go by. The boy in black has lost interest in me. He's whistling and dancing on the corner, involved only with himself.

He is as strange and terrible and beautiful as someone from another star system. I hurry away, my heartbeat thudding in my throat.

Eventually I stop in a bakery and ask for directions to my mother's house. A young woman tells me, explaining about public transportation, the difficulty in getting a taxi so late in the afternoon, and the quickest way to walk that far. A man in the back room keeps interrupting her, shouting, "Call her a taxi!"

She finally does, and to her apparent surprise one arrives shortly. It occurs to me as the taxi climbs steep hills that my mother is probably home and worried about me.

But I'm wrong. I run up the steps and let myself inside her house, calling out for her. No answer. Just in time I remember that I must turn off the alarm system, and I tap out my birthday on the keypad. The red light goes out.

I need desperately to talk to someone about what has just happened to me. At my grandmother's house, I could tell her or anyone, and they would listen and comment. Eventually my adventure would become a teatime story. I reach for the phone and stop.

I am in my mother's house. I'll tell her.

But I don't. When she comes home, she's nervous and exhausted, telling me things I don't understand about her business and people I haven't met. I help her fix dinner and we eat in the dining room, overlooking her small side garden.

Over dessert, Mother says, "How's everything in Seattle? After Olivia's funeral, or whatever you call that ceremony on Puget Sound?"

I wince, remembering the ceremony. Mother has made it sound like some sort of money-saving disposal service. "Everybody misses her," I say.

"She was a nice woman," Mother says. She pours herself more coffee. "Well, cancer is bad. So how did you spend your afternoon? Did you look around my garden? I have a man who comes in several times a month to check it over."

I blink. She switched from cancer to her garden so fast that I didn't have a chance to change mental gears. "Your garden is nice," I say. "Olivia liked working with flowers."

Mother raises her hand. "Let's not dwell on Olivia," she says. "I can't stand rehashing everything. What's done is done. Life is for the living."

She sounds like a fortune cookie. I can't look at her. I can't think of anything else to talk about, either. In a way she's right — there's no point in talking on and on about Olivia's death. I'm always wishing that life would start happening to me. Well, it's never going to if all I do is relive what's already over with.

"Did you have trouble with the alarm system when you got home?" Mother asks.

"No. Did you have the same one the last time I was here? It seems different."

"This is a new one," she says. "Much better than the other."

"Did someone burglarize you?" I ask. "You never mentioned it on the phone or in your letters."

"Not since you were here last time," she says. She stacks our plates, then drinks the last of her coffee.

"But you had been before?" I ask.

Her gaze bounces off me. "Who hasn't?" She picks up the stack of plates and starts for the kitchen.

I follow. "Yolande's old computer was stolen," I say. "The police didn't find it."

"The police never find anything," Mother says, her voice sharp and too loud, as if she were hoping that the police were somewhere nearby, listening.

"Didn't they find what was stolen from you, either?" I ask.

"I didn't bother calling them," she says. She puts the stack of dishes down on a tile counter with such force that I'm afraid she might have cracked one. "What's the point? They never locate anything that's been stolen."

"But don't you have to tell them so you can collect the insurance?" I ask.

She turns her head, her hair swinging on her shoulder. "If I'd told the insurance company, they would have raised the rates, even for my fire insurance."

I think about this. She seems so unprotected, somehow, in spite of the grilles and the alarm.

"We have to learn to take care of ourselves," she says.

"Yes," I say. Does she think that I can do that?

Later Grandmother calls to talk to both of us. When my turn comes, I want to tell her about the dancer, but I don't. Instead, I mention where we had lunch. Mother, listening, still doesn't know that I didn't go directly home from her office.

Afterward Mother and I watch television for an hour. The phone rings constantly for her. Are these callers her friends? I can't tell. She seldom says anything personal.

After the last call she takes out a stack of papers, excuses herself, and goes to her room to work. I go into my bedroom, turn out the light, and sit by the window, clenching my fists. I don't know what's wrong with me.

Darkness has fallen on the garden outside, and the lights at the top and bottom of the steps are on. Wind tosses branches against the house, rattling under the eaves. An elderly couple descend the hillclimb, and after a while, a solitary shadow stops outside Mother's low fence.

Who is it? Who watches from the dark?

The figure moves on, slowly climbing. Probably he was only someone who needed to rest a moment.

I go to bed, but wake after a fractured dream of Colleen and her father.

Eventually Colleen will move in with Grandmother. Then her terrible childhood will become one of the teatime stories, with a beginning, a middle, and an end. But I will still be the one whose history is incomplete. Why is my mother here instead of there?

Or why am I not here? Not until now, that is. Am

I welcome now because I am at last old enough to take care of myself?

I wake again, sitting upright, listening. I've heard something. The tinkle of broken glass. I'm on my feet, scurrying for the window. There's no one on the steps or in my mother's front yard. I run across the hall and open her door.

"Mother, I heard glass breaking!"

She's up instantly. I hear something heavy slide off her nightstand. "Where?" she says. "Here?"

"Not in front," I say. "I looked."

She opens the curtains at both her windows and looks out. "It's next door," she says angrily. "Somebody is breaking in. The owners are out of town."

"Shall I call the police?" I ask.

"No. I'll handle it." She shoves open the window and leans out as far as she can, close to the bars.

My hair feels as though it's standing on end. I clamp my hands over my mouth so I don't utter the cry that chokes me.

"Stop right where you are," I hear my mother say to someone outside. "I have a gun and I'll use it."

I am stunned, staring, barely breathing.

Mother taps something metallic against the bars outside her window. The clanging must echo for a block. "One more move and I'll shoot you," Mother cries.

I hear footsteps running on cement and disappearing finally. Mother closes the window and sighs. "Little creep," she says. She switches on her bedside lamp and picks up her phone.

"Are you calling the police?" I ask. My mouth is dry.

"Of course not," she says. "What would be the point? They won't nail a board over the broken window. I'm calling the neighbor's security company. They'll come out right away and do whatever's necessary. I told the family they should have bars like mine put up. Safety doesn't have to be unattractive."

I can't take my eyes off the gun in her hand. She put it on her bed, and it gleams an oily midnight blue against the white spread. When she finishes her conversation, she hangs up and lifts the gun again. "Why are you staring at it? It won't bite."

She pushes at the cylinder and removes the bullets, then hands the gun to me. "Here. Take it. It can't hurt you."

I put my hands behind my back. "I've never seen one this close before. Grandmother doesn't have a gun."

Mother doesn't respond to that. Instead, she drops the bullets back into the cylinder and snaps it in place.

"Have you ever fired it?" I ask.

She looks at me. "At the gun range. But I don't make a habit of firing off a few shots with a Colt Thirty-eight Special every night to amuse myself, if that's what you're thinking. It's protection. If your grandmother lived alone, she'd get one, too."

She's wrong. I've heard Grandmother speak when she's angry. The sharp contempt in her voice would stop a burglar cold.

"Where did you get the gun?" I ask.

She shrugs. "You can buy anything in this town."

I know.

Mother lays the gun on the night table. "It's late," she says. "You'd better go back to bed."

"I don't think I can sleep," I say. "I'm still scared."

"Put the whole thing out of your mind," she says. "There's no point in dwelling on what happened. The men will come and board up the window and that will be that. It's over."

"Maybe the burglar will come back. Maybe . . ."

"Nonsense," Mother says. She gets into bed and reaches toward her lamp. "He's miles away, breaking into somebody else's house. Why do you care? It's not our problem anymore. Good-night, Gray."

I don't have a choice, so I go back to my own room and shut the door. Once again I look out the window at the tossing shadows. Is someone out there?

In bed, I hug the pillow and whisper, "I'm so scared."

I'm tempted to call Grandmother and tell her what happened. She'd repeat the story of Yolande's burglary, and when she was done, I'd feel better because, after all, we were not hurt and Yolande got a new computer and Markie probably bit the burglar. Everything turned out all right in the end.

I need to hear that, but I can't call this late. My pillow is silent and offers me no comfort.

So maybe I can't take care of myself after all. And Mother will reject me again.

❧ *Chapter 11* ❧

On Saturday morning we leave the house early, but we don't spend much time sightseeing. I can tell that Mother is impatient.

Finally she says, "Why don't we go shopping? We'll get you some new clothes and pick up a few things for your room."

I look down at my jeans. "I guess I should have brought something better," I say, embarrassed.

"You look fine," she says, but she's absent-minded, striding ahead rapidly. "Girls your age never have enough to wear, though. And wouldn't you like a stereo in your room? I thought teenagers couldn't get through the day without their music."

I remind her that she gave me a stereo set last Christmas.

"But that's in Seattle," she says.

Is she assuming that I'm going to move here? I have to set her straight. "I don't need a stereo for just a few days."

She doesn't say anything more. I wonder what she's thinking. Is she going to pressure me about this? Why does she want me here?

We end up in a department store buying clothes. She's fun now, more like Colleen than a mother, rummaging through the racks and holding up one garment after another, laughing at some, nodding at others. When we leave, both of us carry bags stuffed with new clothes for me.

She signals a taxi in front of the store. I cram all my bags under one arm and reach to open the door for her. At that instant all the bags she's carrying slide from her arms to the street. She scrambles for her purse. While I'm helping her load up again, a man slips between us and the taxi, tosses his briefcase inside, starts to crawl in after it, and shouts an address at the driver.

His rudeness infuriates me! How could he treat my mother that way? I drop my bags and reach around him, grabbing the handle of his briefcase. "This is *our* taxi!" I shout, and I throw his briefcase on the street.

He's yelling, I'm yelling, Mother is laughing, and the taxi driver snarls, "Get outta here, you bum," at the man.

An old man in a long white robe hobbles up, bellowing something about corporations ruining the Spaceship Earth. A ragged woman pushing a cart follows him. "Fire!" she shouts. "Fire and rape!" She hits the old man with a plastic bag filled with vegetables.

"Where to?" the taxi driver yells over the racket.

Mother gives her office address and the driver takes off with a screech of tires. "It gets worse all the time, lady," he says.

But we're laughing in the back seat, leaning against each other and whooping.

"You're like your grandmother in a way," Mother says.

"Except she wouldn't have yelled the way I did," I say.

"Right. She would have frozen him stiff with a few quiet comments about his manners, his upbringing, and his level of intelligence." Mother hugs me. "I'm glad you're noisier. I'm glad you're a little bit like me."

But I'm not, I think. The man's rudeness caught me off guard. Ordinarily I would have let him take the taxi.

I'm not like anybody.

"Why are we going to your office?" I ask.

"I need to check up on a couple of things," she says. "It won't take a minute, and then we'll have lunch."

But it takes more than a minute, and finally Mother tells me to leave the bags with her and find a place to have lunch.

She grins at me. "Then fight your way into another

taxi and wait for me at home. I should be there by three. We'll eat out tonight, and maybe see a movie. Okay?"

I nod, but I sigh inwardly.

I find a small place to eat, one that doesn't look busy. While I have lunch, I pull my map out of my purse and study it, tracing a possible sightseeing route with my finger.

And then, without really wanting to, I find the intersection where I saw the dark dancer.

Is he there every day? I'd like to watch him again, but from a safe distance. To whom does he sell his chains and watches? And the other things that he bragged he could find?

Colleen would love hearing about him. So would Grandmother and the others. I could count on Belle to say something funny. I owe it to them to find him and watch.

I pay my check, leave, and carefully follow the map. It takes longer than I thought, and I'm tired by the time I find the shabby neighborhood on the busy street again.

From a block away I see him, the strange boy in black. He dances between people on the sidewalk, stopping now and then, flapping his coat, laughing and posturing. Most people stare. A few speak to him. Some do business with him, shielded by the coat.

This is stupid. He could be dangerous.

I see the same girl, the one who wore the purple

sweater yesterday. Now she wears pants open at the side and laced up, with bare skin showing. She watches the boy. I'm too far away to tell if she's smiling.

He sees me. I know it the instant he looks in my direction. I'm already backing away when he calls out, "Goldilocks!"

He struts toward me, light on his feet but not feminine. He's all in black again, but this time his running clothes have a thin gold stripe on the legs.

"So the bears didn't get you," he says, laughing. He flips open his coat, showing me the chains. "Dancer knew you change your mind, little girl tourist."

He scares me, yet I can't leave. I shove my hands in my pockets, lift my chin, and scowl. "I had to come this way," I say.

Even his golden eyes are filled with the wonderful, bell-like laughter. "Dancer know you speak the truth," he says. "You *had* to come this way." He twirls, his arms weaving, then steps closer to me than he was before.

"Tell Dancer what you want, little girl," he says softly. "I get anything for you because you have all that wild, pretty hair."

I shake my head. "I don't want anything. No chains — nothing."

"Everybody want something," he says. "You scared to ask?"

"No," I say. I'm losing my fear of him. People

passing us glance at both of us. Some smile. Most don't.

"You want a nice stereo set?" he asks. "Maybe a television set, still in its box?" His eyes glow. "Maybe this sweet child want a nice new dolly?" He laughs and turns, his fingers trailing in the air. "Dancer can get you a doll," he says. His fingers trace a doll shape in front of me.

A man passing, hearing this, laughs aloud.

Dancer laughs, too. "Come on, Goldilocks, tell me what you want."

I'm fighting a blush that wants to spread across my face. "I don't want anything," I say, angry now.

He cocks his head. "Nothing? Not even a teddy bear?"

I bite my lip. How dare he treat me like a child. "What I want not even you could get."

He was about to twirl around again, but he stops. His eyes flare beneath his long lashes. "Oh?" he says, drawling the word. "You think Dancer lie to you? I can get anything for you, little girl. Anything."

"How about a gun," I say.

The word pops out of my mouth like a toad. A gun? I've never even thought of having a gun. My mother's gun horrifies me.

I have all of Dancer's attention now. He seems to grow taller. "What a baby like you want with a gun?" he asks, his voice quiet, lower now, rumbling.

I jerk my gaze away for a moment, more than simply frightened, determined that he won't see it in my eyes. "If I don't ask where you'd get a gun, why should you ask why I want it?"

He laughs. "My, my. Little girl tourist scares me. Maybe she got sharper teeth than the bears do."

I don't say anything. My hands would be trembling if they weren't in my pockets.

He stares at me without blinking. Finally he says, "What kind of gun you want?"

"A Thirty-eight," I say. "A Colt Special. And bullets, too."

He bends over, laughing again. When he looks up, his eyes are narrow, like a cat's. "Can't have one without the other," he says. "How you planning to pay for this cannon, Goldilocks?"

Now he's got me. The game is over, but I don't want to surrender. I shrug, hoping I've carried it off. "If you really had one, you'd quote me a price up front," I say, remembering all the dickering I learned in the flea market with Minette. "I'll go somewhere else."

And I turn away, determined not to run — but running anyway. I look back to see if he's following me, but the crowd is greater now. He's vanished. No one stares at me, and I marvel at this.

But there are places in Seattle, too, where no one would stare at me after seeing me talking to the dancer.

My heart doesn't stop thudding until I'm blocks away and lost again. I stop to read my map, discover I've run in the right direction, and keep going. I look back but I never see the dancer. Once, though, I think I see the girl, and I hurry.

Mother isn't home when I get there, not that I expected her. I remember to shut off the alarm, and go to the kitchen to fix myself something to eat.

I'm shaking all over and sick with worry. There's no way I can eat the sandwich I've made, so I dump it in the garbage.

What possessed me to play that stupid game with the boy? I must be going crazy. Just because I bullied a man who was trying to steal our taxi doesn't mean I can take on someone like the strange and sinister boy on the street corner. I let myself get angry because he was teasing me, treating me like a child.

No, this isn't a story I can tell at teatime. Grandmother would think I had lost my mind.

I call Grandmother, but not to talk, only to ask questions.

"What's been going on since I left?" I say. "Have you heard from Colleen?"

"She left here a few minutes ago," Grandmother says. "She went to the flea market with Minette and they sold every scrap."

"It must not be too hot there," I say. "More people show up if it's cool, as long as it doesn't rain. How's everybody getting along?" I need to know how everybody's handling Olivia's absence, but I can't say it.

Grandmother knows what I mean. "We miss Olivia terribly," she says. "And Gip, too. But Belle's gentleman friend has persuaded her to go out to dinner with him, so she's running around pressing clothes and primping and driving us all slightly mad."

I can hear Belle's laughter, and I laugh, too. "What are the rest of you going to do tonight?" I ask. I'm homesick.

"TV looks good," Grandmother says. "But Yolande's deserting us for a barbecue with some of her writer friends."

And Aaron, I want to ask. How is he?

But Grandmother doesn't read my mind this time, so I hang up a few minutes later without learning about him.

I hate being in this house alone. I wouldn't want to live here, but I don't want to go back without Mother begging me to stay. I need to know that she wants me.

When Mother gets home she tells me about the office. We're in her bedroom. She's changing clothes, and she looks up at me. "You're awfully quiet. What's wrong?"

"Why do you want me to move here now?" I ask. "Why now and not before?"

Her face goes white. She sits down on the bed. "I always wanted you here," she says. "Why would you think I didn't?"

I don't want to argue with her, but I need answers, and I won't get them if she says only what she thinks I want to hear. "I know you didn't want me here before, but I don't know why. Was it because you had to work? Sometimes I thought it was that."

"That's part of it. You were better off living with your grandmother than here and going through the day-care thing."

"I haven't needed day-care for a long time," I say.

We're looking away from each other as if we're embarrassed by the conversation. I guess we are.

She sighs and lets the blouse she's holding fall from her hands. "Not needing day-care and being able to take care of yourself are two different things. You're old enough now to manage situations you couldn't have handled two or three years ago." She laughs suddenly. "Like that man who tried to take our taxi. I'll bet he's still furious."

If she knew how stupid I'd been with the dancer, she wouldn't think I can take care of myself. Except that somehow I did. I actually did. I went back to look at him, I even talked to him, and I got away.

I straighten up a little. "I guess you're right. I can take better care of myself now."

"And you're old enough to appreciate the excitement of a city like this," she says. "It's time now for you to step out and live a little. You'll be fifteen soon — it's such a wonderful age."

"I don't exactly live in a padded box in Seattle," I say.

"I know, I know," she says. "But I grew up in that house, too. I even went to your high school. Nothing prepared me for life. Your grandmother doesn't have the slightest idea what goes on in the real world. She lives in the safe past. Maybe she manages to protect herself better that way, but she doesn't really live, either. Teatime every day." Mother shakes her head, exasperated. "All those stories, told over and over again. Linen tablecloths and polished silver. People haven't lived that way for years and years."

"Except at Grandmother's house," I say.

Mother reaches for me, drops her hands before they touch me. "I'm sorry. I know how much you love her. But you need more than the company of old women now. Otherwise you'll go out into the world the way I did, without a clue about how to take care of yourself or stand up to people."

Well, she's told me why she wants me here now instead of years ago. But why am I standing here thinking that she hasn't told me the most important reason? And she won't, not unless I catch her, the real her. And I can't unless I discover where to look.

She's left the room, buttoning the blouse, and calls out to me from her bathroom that we ought to leave soon. "Pick one of the new outfits we got for you today," she says. "We're going to have a wonderful time."

I look at her bedside table. Carefully, so she won't hear, I pull out the drawer and look at the gun. Is that taking care of yourself? Would Grandmother think so? Would Colleen?

We go out to dinner, see a movie, and return to the house before ten. The wind is blowing again. As we climb the steps, our shadows are caught and tangled with the tossing tree shadows, and my spine seems to curl with fright.

Once inside, with all the lights downstairs burning,

I feel at ease again. Mother goes to the kitchen to cut slices from the chocolate torte we bought after we left the theater. I, at the living room window, look at my reflection in the window. I seem taller. Older. I'm growing up.

A shadow moves beyond the glass and I leap back, holding my breath. Someone is outside the house.

I step forward and yank the curtains closed, then turn to leave the room, my mouth already open to shout for Mother.

Someone taps on the grille outside the front door as I pass through the hall. A mouse would tap harder. I stop to listen. Did I hear it? No.

"Goldilocks," someone says quietly.

The dark dancer has found me. How could I have believed that he wouldn't?

He only says my name once. He knows I heard him.

Mother is humming in the kitchen. Plates clink on the counter.

My fingers are numb but quick. I unlock the door and open it, knowing I'll be safe behind the locked grille.

"Dancer find you," he murmurs. He is dark in the dark, but his eyes shine.

"What do you want?" I ask, keeping my voice low.

He shakes one side of his coat. His hand is in the pocket, deep inside. "I got what you want," he says. "Dancer been laughing all afternoon. Little girl like you with a gun. But I do what I promise."

He pulls his hand from his pocket and I see a dull

127

gleam and then it's gone. Together his hands sketch something in the air.

A dollar sign.

"This cost you many bucks, little girl tourist," he says. "But maybe, if you tell me why you want it, I cut you a deal."

I start to close the door. My tongue has stuck to the roof of my mouth.

"Hey, hey, Goldilocks," he says, a little louder now. "You shut that door and I have to yell for your mama and papa. Maybe they don't know that their little darling wants her a cannon to play with. Maybe they *need* to know."

"I changed my mind," I say. "I don't want it." My voice is squeaky. Why did I look for him today? Why did I talk to him? How could I have been so stupid?

He's not smiling. The light from the hall falls on his polished ivory face.

"Dancer, he know people who be very interested in the little girl tourist who wants a gun," he says, his voice soft. "Maybe Dancer should tell them before that bad child put herself in serious trouble. Maybe they can talk to her mama and papa and stop her in time. Unless, of course, that bad child can persuade the Dancer he don't need to worry about her. Reward him, say."

I slam the door and lock it.

Mother is standing behind me holding a plate in each hand. "Who was that?" she asks.

🌿 *Chapter 12* 🌿

I tell Mother everything. She listens without saying a word, and then she tells me that I've acted like a child.

"Whatever possessed you to do something that silly?" she asks. Her face is pale, her eyes glittering. "This isn't a dream world. There are ugly people all over the place, people just waiting for someone like you, someone who's been too sheltered."

She moves about, peering out of windows, checking locks even though we are protected inside the ornate bars.

"Are you going to call the police?" I ask, terrified that she will, terrified that she won't.

Grandmother would. She'd already be on the phone. I'd have to repeat my humiliating story to officers who'd stare at me. They'd search for the boy, come back and lecture me, then search again. It would take weeks — months! — of hearing her, Minette, and Yolande — even Colleen — telling and retelling the night's activities before I'd be able to listen without cringing.

Mother shakes her head. "What good would it do to call the police?" she asks. "They won't bother looking for him — not unless he does something worse than trying to sell you a gun."

She puts down the plates with our dessert, picks them up again and says, "I've lost my taste for chocolate."

She takes the plates to the kitchen. I follow, miserable and ashamed. "I'm really sorry," I say. "I know what I did was stupid. What are you going to do? The boy could still be out there."

She looks thoughtfully at the kitchen window. The shade is pulled, hiding the bars outside.

"He's probably gone," she says. "But that doesn't mean he won't come back to harass us, particularly since he has the idea that we might give him money. We'll just leave."

"Leave?" I ask. "Now? In the dark?" The thought scares me.

She's going through the phone book she took from the shelf under the kitchen phone. "Of course we won't leave now," she says. "We can't take the chance at night. But he can't get in here, and we'll be gone first thing in the morning."

"Where are we going?" I ask. I have visions of her taking me back to Seattle in disgrace.

"To San Diego," she says. She's punching out numbers on the phone, and while I stand there, helpless and sick with self-disgust, she makes reservations for us on an eight o'clock flight tomorrow morning.

"Why?" I ask when she hangs up.

"I've been meaning to go," she says. She opens the cupboard and takes out a glass. While she pours water from a refrigerator jug, she says, "The manager I had at my apartment house left last month. One of the tenants has been doing his work, but he's not sure he wants to go on with it. I might be more successful in convincing him to take the job if I talked to him in person."

She drinks her water, offers me some, and when I shake my head, she puts the jug away.

"Where will we stay?" I ask. "In a hotel?"

"No, no," she says. "There's an empty apartment in the building. We can stay there. I always do when I'm in San Diego."

Before we go upstairs she sets the burglar alarm and cautions me about it. "If you come downstairs during the night, don't walk too close to the front door — or the kitchen door, either. And don't open a window on either floor. There are sensors that will trigger the alarm."

"Why do you need the alarm if you have the bars?" I ask.

"I suppose I don't. It makes me feel better, I guess."

It doesn't make me feel better. I lie awake most of

the night. A dozen times I get up and look out the window, careful not to touch it. The shadows on the stairs dance tirelessly. But no one is ever there.

We are on our way to the airport at six-thirty in the morning, each of us carrying a small bag. Mother wears jeans and a long cotton sweater. Her hair is pulled back in a ponytail. She doesn't look young. She only looks exhausted.

I can't stop apologizing for the mess. Finally, in a voice tight with anger, she says, "I never want to hear another word about this. Not one more word. The subject is closed."

I feel even worse. I sit in the terminal with an open book, but I can't concentrate on it. Now there's no chance she'll want me to stay in San Francisco with her. I've shown her that she was wrong to think I could take care of myself.

And the very fact that she believes this makes me want, desperately, to change her mind.

What can I do to convince her that I don't make a habit of attracting the attention of people like the boy in black? That I wouldn't bring chaos into her life?

I try to engage her in conversation, but she's distracted — and bored with me. In spite of this, I can't give up. I am like a puppy, bringing toys to her to see if she will play with me.

Prattling in desperation, I tell her about the old man who spoke to us on the ferry after we scattered Olivia's ashes over the Sound.

Mother stares at me while I speak, then looks around, her glance furtive. "Please," she whispers, "don't bring up something like that here. There's no telling who's listening to you. Just drop it, okay?"

She's ashamed of me. I retreat within my book, swallowing humiliation as if it were scalding water.

In San Diego, she rents a car and drives us to a quiet neighborhood near Balboa Park. We park in front of a small stucco apartment house surrounded with flowers. A row of short palm trees rustles in the warm wind. We walk along a path between the trees and the building's white wall. Mother unlocks an arched door and gestures for me to walk inside ahead of her.

I see a small living room with neat, shabby furniture, and a faded rug on a tile floor. Beyond, a small dining area opens into an even smaller kitchen.

Mother leads the way to a bedroom. The bed is made up with sheets and a spread. In one corner sits a crib, also made up. The spread is embroidered with a lamb and the initials GEJ.

Grayling Elizabeth Jordan.

"Who lived here?" I ask.

Mother, unzipping her suitcase on the bed, looks up. "This was the apartment your father and I had when you were born."

I look around. "Hasn't anybody lived here since?"

"Oh, yes. After your grandfather died, we took you to Seattle for a visit. We sold our furniture before we left because we were going to live in San Francisco, in the house I've got now."

"Did you own this building then?" I ask. "How did you get the furniture back?" I've got goosebumps on my arms. This is scary, like sliding down an icy hill into the past.

"This isn't the same furniture, but it's as close as I could find," Mother says. "And no, we didn't own the building then. I bought it years later. This apartment happened to be empty at the time, so I furnished it to look the way it did when we lived here. Or as close as I could manage, anyway. And I've never rented it."

On the dresser, I see my mother's wedding picture. I've seen a copy of it in Grandmother's album. I pick it up and study my father's face. And my mother's.

I put the picture back and look around again. "What about the cover on the crib?"

"That was yours," she says. "It was in storage, along with the books in the living room, even the dishes and kitchen things. And all the towels and sheets were in storage, too. Everything but the furniture was here when John and I lived here."

"You never told me about this place," I say.

She's unpacked her clothes and hung them in the closet. Now she's taking out my things.

"Mother?" I say. "You never said anything about this apartment."

"What's to tell?" she says. "Here, you finish hanging up your clothes. I'm going next door and ask the man about managing the place. When I get back, we'll take off. The zoo is wonderful. And there's Sea World and other places to see."

She goes out, padding swiftly in her tennis shoes, leaving me alone. I stand by the crib, fingering the spread, running my hands over the smooth sheets, squeezing the fuzzy white blanket.

Water is splashing somewhere. I look out the window and see a fountain in the center of a patio. Flowers bloom everywhere.

I go back to the crib. My father must have stood here watching me, perhaps saying my name. I go back to the dresser and pick up the wedding picture and hug it to my chest. What would I have called him? Daddy? Father? Dad? Pop?

When I hear the front door open, I put the picture back and snatch a skirt up from the bed.

Mother comes in, looking annoyed. "He's out of town and won't be back until tomorrow afternoon," she says.

"You were going to spend the night anyway," I say, trying to soothe her. "Isn't that why we brought pajamas and other clothes?"

"I'd hoped to get back late tonight," she says. "But I always bring clothes with me. You can never be sure of anything."

She's angry at being stuck here. The burden of trying to please her is heavy on me, like a load of rocks. "We can have a good time driving around and looking at everything."

"I suppose," she says.

"Maybe we ought to find a phone and tell Grandmother where we are," I say. "She might call and worry when we don't answer."

"Of course," she says. She picks up the bedroom phone and dials.

Even the phone is connected. It's as if this apartment were waiting for her to come back with me and my father and pick up where they left off. Or perhaps it's a shrine she created. Frightened, I wonder if she's a little bit crazy.

She tells Grandmother briskly that she has business in San Diego and took me along. She doesn't say a word about the boy, the dark dancer who will haunt me now until I find a way of waking up from the nightmare he created.

When she hangs up, I ask her why she didn't tell.

She won't look at me. "I told you I don't want to hear anything more about that incident," she says.

I can't bear this. I didn't want to come to California, or to live with her, either. But now that I can see how much she regrets inviting me, I must somehow make her want me again.

But then what would I do? Would I move to San Francisco with her? Go to school there? Leave Colleen behind, and Grandmother? And Aaron?

I think of Aaron while we are walking through the zoo. I think of him too much. He's probably relieved that I'm out of town, for now he isn't stuck with baby-sitting me while real life goes on in the house, or at least the parts of it that I'm excluded from because I'm too young.

I'm too young for my mother, too. I complicate things, obligate her to change plans, tighten security, even run away.

My mother's very good at running away.

That night we bring Chinese food home and eat it in the kitchen. I ask her again, after a long silence, why she left me in Seattle to be raised by Grandmother.

"It was best," she says, as she always does when I bring up that subject. "For years I never had time for anything but work. You'd have been raised in day-care or by a housekeeper. You're better off in Seattle."

She doesn't say that I *was* better off. She says that I am.

She's made her decision. I can't take care of myself well enough to live with her.

I lie awake in bed again, and when I do manage to sleep, I dream of the dark dancer who tempted me, leading me here to the final rejection. He slips and slides through my nightmares, beckoning, laughing, his long fingers twined with gold chains.

On Monday we visit Sea World in the morning and Old Town in the afternoon. While we sit on a bench I ask Mother why she left Seattle on that particular day.

"Not here," she says. "People are always eavesdropping."

"No one is near us," I say. The closest people, two middle-aged women taking pictures of one another, are on the other side of the courtyard.

Mother sighs and gets to her feet. "Where do you want to have dinner tonight?" she asks.

"I don't care."

"I have to see my tenant this afternoon and I don't know how long that will take," she says. She is striding away, and I have to run a little to keep up. "Maybe we could eat in this wonderful soup and salad place. Does that sound good?"

"Anything's fine," I say.

In the car, I ask her again. "Why did you leave that day?" I say. "I know that something happened the night before. They — Grandmother and Minette — talk about how you came home covered with mud and without your car. Nobody knew why you left. You didn't tell them what happened."

She shields her eyes from the sun and shakes her head impatiently. "What's the point of dragging up the past? What good will it do anybody?"

But my story has no end, I want to cry. No one knows why I've been growing up there. No one knows what happened to you that night that made you decide to leave me behind. The story of baby Grayling only has a beginning and a middle.

I don't say anything more, however. Her defenses are up, thick and tight. She'll answer all my questions with questions of her own.

At the apartment, she leaves me alone while she hunts down the tenant. I go out the kitchen door and cross the patio to stand beside the fountain. The water is warm, running over my fingers. I cup my hand and catch some, but it trickles away.

At my feet I see a plastic cup. I catch water in that, filling it to the brim, thinking of Colleen and me catching rain for so many years, as Grandmother and Minette did before us.

Did my mother ever catch the rain?

I go inside and call Grandmother. Mother won't mind.

The phone rings and rings before Yolande finally answers, breathless and half-laughing.

"It's Gray," I say. "What's going on?"

"We're all in the garden picking strawberries," she says.

She asks what I've been doing and I tell her. "I won't make Grandmother come in," I say. "Everything's fine and I'm enjoying myself. I'll call tomorrow."

I say good-bye while Yolande is still protesting and offering to go get Grandmother in from the garden.

Tonight the mint will smell fresh and crisp, down in the woods by the creek. And the moon will turn the last of the clouds to silver. The owl will call but I won't be there to hear him.

The front door bangs and Mother hurries in. "There. That's done. We'll be able to get a late flight home. Start packing, Gray, while I make our reservations. Then we'll eat at the airport."

I want to go home to Seattle, not San Francisco. But not until I learn why my mother left me behind with my grandmother.

❦ *Chapter 13* ❦

During breakfast on Tuesday, I ask Mother if she'll show me the high school. I don't want to see it, but I'm still trying to undo her rejection. If I try hard to please her . . .

She doesn't look at me. Sipping juice, eyes on a small TV, she says, "There won't be time. I'm going to the office early, and you'll be flying back this afternoon."

"You made my reservation already?" I ask, startled.

"I will as soon as I'm done eating," she says. No apologies. No explanations. And no regrets.

But she can't get a reservation for me until the eight-thirty flight this evening. Half of San Francisco is flying to Seattle.

Sighing, she slams down the phone. "You'd better

stay in the house today," she says. "No, come to the office. We'll find something for you to do. And bring your suitcase. I'll have one of the secretaries call the airline every hour or so to see if there's a cancellation."

"Mother," I say. My voice sounds like a little girl's. My throat hurts because I'm trying not to cry. "Please tell me the truth before I leave."

She stares at me, color burning her cheekbones. "What are you talking about?"

"Why did you run away that day?"

She gets to her feet and snatches at the plates. "I didn't run away. Did your grandmother give you that idea? She romanticizes everything, she and Minette and . . ."

"Olivia," I say, finishing her sentence. "Nobody's romanticizing anything. But they try to find reasons. And we don't have a reason for the day you left me. They told me that all you said was that you were going. They didn't know what happened to you the night before, but they think that it made you want to go to San Francisco alone."

Mother's back is to me, stiff and unyielding. "I've explained a dozen times to you over the years," she says. "I don't know why you can't accept the simple truth. *They've* done this to you with all their tea parties and gossip. Idle old women with nothing to do but speculate about other people's lives."

"That's not fair," I say. "You're calling them lazy, and they aren't! Grandmother runs a company, too, just like you, but she does it from the house. Minette buys and sells things. Belle still lectures and consults with other doctors. Yolande writes two books a year."

But Mother doesn't hear me. She's slamming dishes around, her face flaming. "I always hated listening to them," she says. "Living in the past, laughing over rubbish that happened years ago, talking about dead people as if they expected them to walk in any minute, bringing up ancient divorces and old quarrels and lawsuits — it drove me crazy. They never get *on* with anything!"

"That's not true!" I cry. "They talk about those things until they make sense, until they understand. Until they can bear it! Someday they'll talk about how Olivia couldn't stand the pain anymore and made them promise to help her fall asleep . . ."

"Stop it!" she shouts. Her face is white with shock. "Don't you dare say something like that! It's not true and you're going to make trouble for everybody if you don't keep quiet."

I meet her gaze. "It's not a lie," I say.

She covers her face with both hands. "I can't believe they'd expose you to something like that." Her hands drop and she stares at me. "You shut up about it, you hear me? Don't ever tell anybody about it."

My sigh seems to come from my feet. "I wouldn't do that," I say, trying to be patient with her as if *she* were the child. "I know better. But it's something that we'll be able to talk about someday, and we'll feel better afterward."

"Go pack your things," she says. "I have to leave for the office."

But I wait while she phones for a taxi to come to the foot of the steps, and when she hangs up, I say, "Why did you leave me behind? What happened to you?"

"Oh, all right!" she shouts. "Have it your own way. Then you can take the story back to Seattle and tell the old ladies over your teacups. The night before I left I saw him again. Him! The man who ran over your father and killed him."

I can't breathe for a long moment. "Where?" I ask finally.

Her face is white and cold, like stone. "I'd gone out to run some errands late in the evening. I saw him in the grocery store. I recognized him instantly. His hair had grown out again — he'd cut it before he showed up in court — it was long and kinky again, bushing around his face. And his smile — the gap between his teeth. He actually smiled at me!"

"What did you do?" I ask. My hands are clenched into fists.

"I ran out to my car, but he followed me. I got lost, and always, there were those headlights behind me. Always."

"Are you sure it was him?" I ask.

"Yes! No! I couldn't think straight. Finally I turned out my headlights so I'd be harder to follow. I didn't touch the brakes, because of the brake lights, not even at stop signs. It must have been midnight by then. I found the other side of the tree farm — you know, that back road that slants off the freeway access road. I speeded up and turned off on it as fast as I dared, and then I left the car and ran through the woods."

"Did anyone follow?"

"I don't know. I stopped to listen many times, but the woods are full of noises. When I smelled the mint by the creek I knew I was almost home."

"But why didn't you tell Grandmother?" I cry. "She would have called the police and told them he — or *some*body — was following you. She said the police hated him as much as the family did."

"What good would it have done?" Her voice is anguished. She's weeping now. "What earthly good? They couldn't do anything to him even when he killed your father! Don't you understand? In court, his lawyer made me sound like a lunatic. I'd been taking pain pills the day your father died because I'd twisted my ankle the day before — that's why he drove me to the store — and the lawyer found out and said I was a woman on drugs when I saw your father killed, so how could anybody believe what I said. The doctor gave me those pills! I wasn't drugged out of my mind!"

She wipes her eyes on a paper towel. "That man went free on the charge of killing your father. And his sentence was suspended for robbing the store. He got away with *every*thing."

"He was killed in prison years later," I say. "He got what he deserved eventually."

She looks at me as if I'd lost my mind. "You don't understand," she says. "I didn't know then what was going to happen a long time afterward."

"Belle says what goes around comes around. We just have to wait. Somebody killed the man who killed my father."

"That's a coincidence," Mother says. Her voice is bitter, her face twisted. "Do you expect that to console me for what I lost?"

I shake my head. "No. But maybe if you'd talk about it, you'd feel better. You could come home with me and tell Grandmother and Minette." I look straight at her. "But you still haven't answered me. Why did you leave me behind?"

"I felt as if I couldn't escape him and other men like him. As if they'd be showing up for the rest of my life, grinning, watching me, following me. How could I learn to run a business and raise a child both, when I never knew when someone like him would cross my path. You were helpless and you made me vulnerable."

She's crying again, so hard that I don't think she'll be able to stop. "All my real courage died with your father," she says.

I look at the bars on the kitchen window, and then I put my arms around her and hug her, hard. "Don't cry, Mama," I say. "Come home with me."

She clutches me. "I can't," she says. "Don't you see that your grandmother's way isn't my way? I can't live my life with too much time to think, dawdling as if I were floating in a puddle of warm water the way she does."

"Actually," I say, tears in my eyes and a smile beginning to curl my lips, "it's more like a puddle of warm tea."

We're laughing and crying at the same time, hugging each other. I can never let her know how much her raw fear has shocked me. Her awful, senseless fear.

Suddenly Mother says, "The taxi driver! I'll run down the steps and tell him to wait while you pack. Hurry!"

I rush upstairs to grab clothes and stuff them into my suitcase. I hear the door open again and Mother calls out, "Are you ready? He's furious and this will cost me a fortune."

I run down. She's pulling on her suit jacket. Her eyes are red, but she's smiling.

"Maybe you could visit me at Christmas," she says as we start down the steps toward the waiting taxi. "I've always gone to Seattle. Maybe you're old enough to spend the holiday here, away from home."

"Maybe," I say.

When we reach her office she finds me a place to sit, introduces me to the secretary who will try to get me an earlier reservation, and gives me money. "If it gets too boring, you leave for a while and do some shopping," she says. "Just keep in touch."

And she disappears behind a door where a dozen people wait for her. She's started her race through the day, fleeing the shadows that she thinks pursue her.

The first time the secretary tries, she gets me a canceled seat on an afternoon plane. I leave the office then and find my way to Golden Gate Park, where I walk until I'm tired.

I'm back at the office by two. Mother, carrying my suitcase, walks down to the street with me. She opens the taxi door and bends inside to kiss my forehead.

"Take care of yourself," I tell her, and I mean it. She doesn't know how vulnerable she is.

She smiles. "Stay out of trouble at the airport," she says, laughing. "Don't talk to strangers."

"I know, I know," I say. "Don't make eye contact with peculiar people. That's what Grandmother's always telling me."

I look back at her when we drive away, but she's already striding toward the building entrance.

Now, when she can't see me, I cry for her.

❧ *Chapter 14* ❧

I'm surprised that Yolande is waiting for me at the airport gate, her face pale and her hair coming loose from its bun again. She hates to drive far, and she especially hates the late afternoon traffic on the freeway. Minette was supposed to pick me up — at least, that had been the plan.

"What's wrong?" I ask as soon as I'm within Yolande's hearing.

"Only everything," she says. "We didn't want to worry you on the phone, but Colleen got into it with her father and moved in with us. Dr. Clement showed up this morning, threatening everything he could think of, but you know Garnet. She got rid of him for the time being, but Minette was afraid he'd be back with a collection of lawyers or the police or something, so she decided to stay home and guard

Garnet and Colleen. I'm hopeless at that sort of thing."

The airport crowd streams around us. Yolande still hasn't explained why Colleen and her father "got into it," but this isn't the time or place. "Let's get my suitcase," I say.

I start off almost running, but Yolande stops me. "Don't rush," she says. "I can't face that awful commuter traffic on the freeway, so I'd like to wait a while. Do you want to call home and tell Garnet that you got here all right?"

I laugh a little. "I'll tell her that *you* got here all right," I said. "She's probably more worried about that."

We get my suitcase first, then find a phone. No one answers at home for a long time, scaring me, but then, when I'm ready to hang up, Grandmother says hello in her usual serene voice.

"Grandmother, it's Gray," I say. "I'm at the airport with Yolande and she wants to wait a bit before starting home until the worst of the commuter traffic dies down. She told me that Colleen's there. What happened?"

"I'd rather wait until you get home to explain all that," Grandmother says. "I'm more interested in why you came back so soon. Your mother didn't say much when she called."

I sigh. "That's something else that should wait until I get home," I say. "Is Colleen all right? I can't help worrying."

"She'll be fine," Grandmother says.

"What do you mean, she'll *be* fine?" I ask.

There's a slight pause. "I'm afraid Colleen and that dreadful brother of Fawn's got into a fight. A physical fight, I mean. She says she gave as good as she got, maybe better, and we certainly hope that's true."

"He hit her?" I ask. "Did he hurt her?"

"A little," Grandmother says. "Don't worry. Belle's taking care of her, and we had her checked out at the hospital, too. But please wait until you get home to ask the rest of your questions. Trust me when I tell you that Colleen's in good hands."

"She's there? Can't I say hello?"

"She's asleep in your room and Belle wants her to rest. We'll be waiting for you and see you in good time." And then Grandmother laughs. "Poor Yolande. That traffic is her trial by fire."

We say good-bye and I turn to Yolande. "I seem to have missed Chapter One of the end of the world."

"You missed the whole first half of the book," Yolande says. "It's nearly six-thirty. Let's start toward the car, but don't hurry. And don't expect me to talk when I'm driving."

I'd intended questioning her about Colleen, but Yolande's rule of silence was firm. If she was nervous, or if the traffic was heavy, she wouldn't even answer a direct question.

So I talk on the way home, mostly about the apartment in San Diego and Mother's house on the hill-climb in San Francisco. I'm burdened with the memory of the dark dancer, but I'm not certain I'll ever have enough courage to tell anyone about it. I'm not as comfortable as the other women in the house about admitting my own stupidities. Or maybe I'm the only one who's that stupid.

If Mother didn't tell, then maybe I'd better keep quiet, too.

But I have the ending for the story of my childhood, and that's a sad sort of relief. I wonder what the others will make of it.

At last we're home. Ben sees me in the car and races clumsily down the driveway beside us, bellowing. Grandmother meets me on the porch, and moments later Colleen appears behind her, yawning. She has a huge bruise on the side of her face.

While Grandmother is hugging me, I'm goggling at Colleen.

"Does it hurt?" I ask. "You look awful."

"Thank you so much," she says, pert and sassy now that she's fully awake. She hugs me, too. "Gee, I'm glad you're home."

Belle limps out, massaging her hands together. "Well, here you are," she says to me. "So your mama kicked you out again and you came back to us like a bad penny." And she laughs.

But I wince. She doesn't know that I really *was* kicked out.

Minette has strawberry shortcake waiting in the kitchen, so we sit around the table eating and smiling at each other.

151

"I'm glad to be back," I say. "So now tell me what happened."

Everybody looks at Colleen — after all, it's her story.

"Sunday morning I decided to take the bus to my mother's," she says.

"By yourself?" I interrupt.

"I would have taken her . . ." Yolande begins.

Grandmother raises her hand. "Let Colleen tell it," she says.

"I've made so much trouble for all of you," Colleen says. "And now everything is even worse. But at the time I thought I'd be doing Yolande a favor if she didn't have to drive me into town. So I went, but my dad and Fawn thought I was going to church. Anyway, while I was gone, *they* took off for the tennis club, leaving Lance home to wait for me."

"Even though they knew what he'd done to you before when the two of you were alone," I say bitterly.

Colleen shrugs. "You know my father. He may be a doctor but he's not even half as smart as a termite. Anyway, I walked in and caught Lance in my bedroom. He'd already pried open the lock on my desk drawer where I keep my money and he'd taken it all. And he was stealing my gold bracelet, too."

"What?" I cry. "The one that belonged to your mother?"

Colleen nods. "He had it in his hand, and when he saw me, he stuffed it into his pocket. I saw my desk drawer then, and I knew he had my money, too. So I told him to give everything back. But he started for the door, pushing me so he could get by. And I grabbed his arm. Before I even knew what happened, he'd knocked me down."

My heart misses a beat. "Then what?"

"I grabbed his legs — oh, Gray, I've never been so mad — I grabbed his legs and tripped him. When he fell, I tried to get my stuff out of his pockets, but he kept hitting me. So I kicked him, lots of times, until he finally got up and ran."

"Where'd he go?"

Colleen laughs now. "To his room. He locked himself in, but he still had my stuff, so I called the tennis club and had them page my father. He acted like we were only having a fight the way little kids do, and he wasn't going to come home, but I told him that if he didn't, I'd call nine-one-one. So he came."

Belle snickers. "He's my hero, all right," she says.

"When he got there," Colleen goes on, "he told Lance to give me back my stuff, but Lance says he didn't take anything. He let my father search him, and of course he didn't have my money or the bracelet on him anymore. So I started going through his drawers real quick, and I found two bottles of Dad's booze and some of his credit cards."

"Now pay attention to the next part," Belle says. "Remember, this child is standing there with bruises on her face."

"So," Colleen says, "Fawn starts whining about how Lance had a terrible childhood and his parents didn't love him . . ."

"Small wonder," Minette observes.

"And nothing ever went right for him," Colleen says. "She said that I snub her and Lance, that I'm spoiled and mean and always say things to hurt their feelings. So my father yelled that he'd heard enough, that he's sick of all of us, and he slammed out of the house."

"Leaving you with Fawn and Lance?" I ask, horrified.

Colleen nods. "So I took off, too. I figured it wasn't too healthy for me around there."

"And as soon as the worthy physician came home and discovered that she was gone," Belle goes on angrily, "he decided to come here and check us out. So he knows for certain where she is."

"But Colleen had to go somewhere!" I cry. "He couldn't have expected her to stay in the house with Lance."

"He doesn't reason like that," Belle says. "Or any other way."

"No, he doesn't," Colleen says. "He didn't have a solution for the problem, but he didn't want me making a decision, either."

"Are you going to stay here?" I ask her. "Or are you going to your mother's place?"

"I wouldn't dare go to Mother," Colleen says. "*He* would think up something awful to do to her. And your grandmother said I could stay, even though my father says he's going to make legal trouble for her."

"What legal trouble?" I ask, scoffing at the idea. But something cold slips up my spine.

"Apparently there are all sorts of things he can accuse us of doing," Minette says.

"But why does he want you back?" I demand of Colleen. "It doesn't make sense. If he's going to let Lance stay there because he's Fawn's brother, then he must know that sooner or later you and Lance are going to tangle again." I'm thinking worse things than just their fighting. Lance is truly bad.

"My father only cares about controlling people," Colleen says. "He wants everybody to do what he says, even if it's stupid."

"There's something else," Yolande says slowly, her voice so quiet that I can barely hear her. "He likes chaos. He thrives on it, so he lets situations go on that will end up in a mess. It's exciting to him."

We all look at her. She's thinking of her awful ex-husband.

"Maybe if he comes back, Cornelius will hit him on the head with a rake," I say, and everybody laughs.

It's grown late. The clocks strike nine and I realize how tired I am. "Where am I going to sleep?" I ask.

"I've moved into Olivia's room," Belle says, her voice deceptively bright. "Colleen slept in your bed because I hadn't cleaned my things out of my old room yet. But I took care of that this afternoon, so we're all set."

"Unless Dr. Clement makes Colleen go home," I say.

Grandmother shakes her head. "If he wants a fight, he'll get one," she says. "I've already spoken to my lawyers. I think Dr. Clement will see reason when we explain the alternatives to him. He'd hate for the Child Protective Services to get into this." She smiles at Belle. "And Belle's reminded him about the interest the hospital staff takes in gossip."

But Colleen and I exchange a look, and I know that she's thinking what I'm thinking. Her father is sly and mean. He'll find a way to make trouble for Grandmother and Belle. After all, he managed to get custody of Colleen away from her mother, no matter what he had to do.

But I'm actually too tired to worry tonight. Colleen and I go upstairs together, and for a while she sits on my bed, asking questions about San Francisco. I tell her about the tourist attractions. But in the back of my mind, the dark dancer whirls and laughs. *Little girl tourist, tell me what you want.*

"What's wrong?" Colleen says. "Your face turned pale. Are you all right?"

"I'm worn out," I say. And then to change the subject, I ask, "Has Aaron been around?"

She laughs. "Of course. He shows up every morning and stays until five or six. I never saw anybody work so hard in all my life. Belle says he does it to impress you, but you haven't been here and he works hard anyway. His dad drove over today. He's a nice man. And he's really pleased with what Aaron's done. He said so right in front of all of us. I wish I had a father like that."

I nod and can't help smiling.

"But listen, Gray," Colleen says, lowering her voice even though no one can hear us. "How come you came back so soon?"

"Mother was too busy to spend time with me," I said.

"You didn't want to stay anyway, did you?" she asks. "And you didn't want to move there, either."

"No." But I'm thinking that I didn't want to be returned like something taken back to a department store because it didn't fit. *I* wanted to do the rejecting.

The way she had rejected me when I was a baby.

But that's not what happened! She couldn't take care of a baby and start her life over again and watch out for the man who ran over my father, not all at the same time. I understand that now. She panicked, so she ran away, but she left me behind where she thought I'd be cared for best.

And she saw to it that I got away from the dark boy, the dancer who'd followed me.

But then she rejected me again because I'm still too much trouble.

Colleen is talking and I haven't been listening. But it doesn't seem to matter, because she's walking toward the door and turns now to say, "Get a good night's sleep and dream about Aaron." And she laughs as she closes the door behind her.

When I'm in my pajamas, I open the door so Ben can come and go. I hear Belle's raucous laughter downstairs, Minette's protest and final collapse into giggles, Grandmother's voice rising and falling musically as she scolds Belle for teasing.

I'm home, I think, and I sleep abruptly.

🌿 *Chapter 15* 🌿

The morning is hushed and strange. The sky threatens rain, and there is no wind, so everything seems to wait.

Aaron arrives, sees me watching, and waves. I wave back, but I'm embarrassed. He knows I was watching for him. He might even know that I'm glad to see him in spite of Belle's matchmaking.

Grandmother takes Colleen into town to see lawyers and a social worker. Grandmother is marching ahead like an army to crush Dr. Clement beneath her neat, slender heel.

Belle leaves soon after for a consultation at the hospital. Yolande, coffee cup in hand, strolls toward the dollhouse.

"Now," Minette says to me, "suppose you sit down at the table with me and tell me everything about your trip."

I sit, dawdling over another glass of orange juice, another piece of toast, talking about San Francisco and San Diego, never mentioning the boy who was responsible for my sudden departure.

No, *I* was responsible! I was the one trying to prove a point.

No matter. I can't talk about him and I've got to stop thinking about him. Mother was right to send me back. I need a whole house full of women to keep me from doing stupid things.

Minette pours herself another cup of coffee. "You've decided that you're not moving to San Francisco, then," she says.

"I never wanted to," I say. "But I couldn't think of a way to tell Mother without hurting her." With my forefinger, I trace a damp circle left by my glass.

"But she was hurt anyway, I suppose," Minette says.

"No," I say. "I don't think so. Maybe she was only going through the motions of asking me to move there. You know how it is — you do what you think people expect you to do." I hesitate a moment, then add, "Maybe she doesn't think I'm old enough to get along without a baby-sitter."

That's as close as I can come to saying that I was sent home because I didn't measure up. Because I need too much protecting.

Aaron sticks his head through the kitchen door. "Grayling, I'm going to paint the trim on the second floor this morning. Both your windows are open. Would you mind closing them?"

"You're going back up on the scaffold?" Minette asks. "Should you do that? It's going to rain."

"Not for a while," Aaron says. "Right, Grayling?"

"Right," I say, even though I haven't been outside to test the day against my experience with Seattle summers. I get up and head for the stairs. "I'll shut my windows," I call back.

While I'm upstairs, I check the windows in the other bedrooms, too, but they're all closed.

In Olivia's room — now Belle's — I stand very still and look around. The bed is the same, but it has Belle's quilt on it, and the pile of pillows she made herself. Olivia's dresser has been cleared of her trinkets and Belle's sit there instead. Olivia's chair is gone — Belle's is in its place. The lamps are Belle's.

So where, then, is Olivia?

My eyes fill with tears and I head blindly for the door. How can Belle stand to sleep in here? Is she punishing herself?

I shut the door behind me. Why should she punish herself? Olivia wanted to fall asleep. It was time. And Grandmother helped. There were all those pills in the bottle she dropped.

But what if . . . I clap my hands over my mouth, as if I had been about to speak. I've got to stop doing this to myself. Olivia is safe now, and where she wanted to be.

It's time to go on with my life, the way Grandmother and Minette and Yolande have done. Someday we'll talk about how Olivia asked and Grandmother promised. We'll take the sting out of it.

I go back downstairs, thumping my feet firmly to announce my coming, hoping that somebody will say something to interrupt my train of thought.

Aaron is leaving the kitchen, holding a piece of toast.

"You'll quit if it starts to rain?" Minette asks.

"Can't paint in the rain," he says. He knows she's afraid he'll fall, I think, but he doesn't like people worrying about him.

Grandmother and Colleen come home sooner than expected. "Lawyers are so exasperating," Grandmother says, yanking off her raincoat and tossing it over a chair. "But the social worker was even worse. It will take forever to get all this sorted out, especially since everybody but us wants to make something complicated out of it."

Colleen and I leave Grandmother and Minette to grumble over lawyers and social workers. We take refuge in the living room.

"How did it go?" I ask.

Colleen rolls her eyes. "I don't have a clue what's going on. I told everybody that no matter what, I'm not going back to my father's house. Not even if Lance leaves. Not even if Fawn moves out! I'll run away first. I think that impressed the social worker. She started talking about foster care then, and your grandmother had a fit." Colleen laughs. "You know how she is."

Colleen imitates Grandmother perfectly, getting to her feet, her spine very straight, her chin lifted arrogantly, her eyebrows arched. " 'My dear woman,' your grandmother said, 'what on earth do you think we've been talking about for the last hour?' "

"And?" I ask, fascinated as I always am by the way my grandmother handles annoying people.

"She just walked out the door," Colleen says, snickering. "I followed her. And your grandmother's lawyer, the old one, ran after us, but she wouldn't stop to talk to him. When we got on the elevator, she said, 'For heaven's sake, Bert, don't take up any more of my time with preliminaries. Just get on with it!' "

I laugh. "That's Grandmother. Does she think everything's going to work out? You can stay with us?"

Colleen shrugged. "I don't care what anybody says, I'm not going back to my father. Period."

I take her word for it. And I don't blame her.

We have lunch when Belle gets home. The rain holds off. All of us, including Yolande, take buckets and boxes down to the orchard to pick cherries. We're nearly finished when Grandmother goes back to the house.

According to my watch, it is three-thirty. How does she know?

"Is it time for tea?" Colleen asks from the branch above me.

"Soon," I say. "We'd better get back. I'm sure that it's going to rain. Can't you smell it?"

We gather up our containers of cherries and start for the house. I see Aaron climbing down the scaffold.

"Rain's coming," he calls out to us.

And then the rain begins, falling hard, pelting us.

"It's a honeysuckle rain!" Colleen yells.

She and I put our cherries on the porch and run for the summer kitchen. Aaron sprints ahead, though, and he drags out the box.

"Tell me how to help," he says.

We kneel, setting jars in the right places to catch the rain, and Aaron faithfully carries out our instructions, even though Colleen and I are both shouting at once.

Aaron and I look at each other, rain streaming down our faces, and we smile. He leans toward me, but not close enough. "Would you like to go to another movie tonight?" he asks. "Could you?"

I'm about to shout, "Yes!" when Dr. Clement's car roars up the driveway. He's come to spoil another honeysuckle rain.

"Oh, no, it's my father," Colleen says in a scared little voice. "What am I going to do?"

She and I leave Aaron to catch rain, and we march toward the porch where Grandmother has confronted Dr. Clement.

"Colleen's coming home right now," he yells at Grandmother. When he sees Colleen, he makes a grab for her, but she dodges and runs up the steps.

"My lawyers and the authorities will be in touch with you," Grandmother says. "In the meantime, it's best if Colleen stays here in a more wholesome environment."

At that moment, Belle pushes open the screen door.

Dr. Clement grins. "Wholesome?" he asks. "You think I'm going to leave my daughter in a house with someone who has no regard for precious human life?"

Belle makes a strange, strangled sound, but she stands her ground. Grandmother, even braver, advances on Dr. Clement.

"I'm not going to waste my time asking what you mean," she says. "I've had enough of your . . ."

"I looked through Olivia's hospital records," Dr. Clement tells Grandmother. "Interesting. She left the hospital even though she was scheduled for more treatment."

"Dr. Roderick signed her out!" Grandmother says. She raised her voice a little, and that was a mistake. Dr. Clement knows he has her now, I think.

"Then she conveniently dies shortly after that, in her sleep. And she's cremated, so there can't be an autopsy." He wipes rain away from his eyes and looks at Belle. "Now why do you suppose everybody was in such a hurry to cremate her? I think a number of people might be interested in exactly how Olivia died."

Colleen, standing to the side and a little behind Grandmother, is staring and staring at him. At first her face registered bewilderment. But now it's blazing with rage. Her gaze flicks off me, then fixes on her father again.

"I believe that everyone will agree that this is no

place for Colleen," Dr. Clement says, and he smiles. "Perhaps she'd better get in my car now, and we'll all continue on with our own business, just as if nothing unusual had occurred. Nothing at all."

"No!" Colleen cries. "You want to know what happened to Olivia? Gray told me the whole thing the next day. She told me that she was sitting all alone with Olivia in her bedroom and reading aloud to her when all of a sudden Olivia closed her eyes and stopped breathing. Isn't that so, Gray?"

Dr. Clement looks at me quickly. I am frozen.

"That's why Gray went to San Francisco," Colleen goes on. "She was upset, seeing someone die like that, so her grandmother sent her away for a few days. Isn't that true, Gray?"

I nod. My neck feels stiff.

"She was all alone with Olivia when she died, and it scared her," Colleen says, spitting the words into her father's face. "So don't you dare try to make trouble here. I'll tell everybody every single word Gray told me, everything! All about how Olivia died right in front of her and how upset she was, how she cried and screamed for somebody to help her, but it was too late."

Dr. Clement is staring hard at me. "I was alone with her," I say, and my voice is steady. "She just fell asleep."

His eyes are slits. He makes a sudden grab for Colleen, but she darts behind Grandmother.

"I explained to the social worker about the felon

who lives in your house," Grandmother says, her voice strong and serene again. "Everyone recognizes that he is a danger to Colleen."

"Lance will be moving out," Dr. Clement shouts.

"You can give that information to the woman yourself," Grandmother says. "I'm sure she'll offer you every opportunity to justify your position."

Minette comes to the door then, and she pretends surprise when she sees Dr. Clement. "Garnet," she says to Grandmother, "your lawyer is on the phone. He says he's got good news for you."

Grandmother herds Colleen in the door. I follow them, and Minette follows me. I glance back and see Dr. Clement standing in the rain. Minette closes the door with a neat, final click.

No one has phoned. Minette is grinning. Belle sighs and sits down hard on the hall bench.

Colleen stands at the end of the hall outside the kitchen door. Her face is pale. But suddenly she gives herself an odd little shake, and then she grins and does a crazy jig. "Yippee!" she shouts. "I sassed him back and got away with it!"

The clock in the hall bongs four times, and the clock in the dining room tinkles the echo.

"Tea, thank God," Minette says.

Dr. Clement's car takes off with a roar and we watch him leave through the windows. Aaron comes in, shaking water off himself like a dog.

"Teatime, Aaron," Grandmother calls down the hall to him.

I wonder how much, if anything, he heard.

"I wish I could stay," he says, "but I can't do anything more today." He smiles at me. "The movie. Is it okay?"

"You asked her out again?" Belle says, barking laughter. "I thought you'd ask *me* the next time. I don't eat nearly as much popcorn and I can pay my own way."

"I don't think I should," I tell Aaron. "Colleen's here."

"Gray will go," Belle shouts. "Pick her up at seven-thirty."

After Aaron leaves, Belle and I are alone in the hall for a moment. I bite my lip.

"Don't you dare fold up on me," she whispers. "Stiffen that backbone." Her eyes are bloodshot again. "I'm sorry Colleen involved you. She shouldn't have. I can't imagine what possessed her. But you'd better not panic over me, not again. I saw that look on your face. If you want to do me a favor, you get moving with your life and don't feel sorry for anybody. You understand me? You do what you have to do."

"Like you did." I lick my lips. My mouth is dry and I'm still shaking.

Suddenly Belle throws her arms around me. "Oh, my big, grown-up girl," she whispers. "I can't hold you on my lap anymore."

"Hey, are you guys coming or not?" Colleen complains from the dining room doorway.

"Coming," Belle says. "Quit that hollering."

Grandmother pours tea and Minette passes the cookies. Colleen and I, balancing cups and cookies, linger in the doorway.

"What do you suppose is going to happen next?" Colleen asks Grandmother. "I mean about me?"

Grandmother, stirring sugar into her tea, cocks her head to one side, considering. "Oh, we shall prevail. Have no fear."

"This is going to make the best teatime story someday," Colleen blurts.

Everyone laughs. She's right.

"I've got one," I say suddenly.

Everyone looks at me. I put my tea and cookies down on the buffet. "I know why my mother left Seattle so suddenly."

And even while I'm telling them the end of the story of my infancy, I wonder if I'll ever have the courage to tell them everything about my trip to San Francisco. In a far corner of my mind, the dark dancer mocks me — and my pride.

When I'm done, everyone's tea is cold. I've surprised them.

"But if Norah was being followed, she could have told us," Grandmother says. "We'd have called the police."

Belle makes a rude noise. "What good would that have done?"

"She was half crazy with grief and anger." Minette shakes her head. "Everything happened at once.

Some people can't handle too much at one time. They panic."

Yolande nods. "But still . . ."

Grandmother sighs. "Norah runs after life and passes it by."

More tea is prepared. This time Colleen and I sit next to the kitchen window and watch the rain fall while the women in the other room talk about the day Olivia rescued a kitten from the tallest fir tree in the woods.

Gradually, when they've recovered from their shock, bit by bit, they'll bring up my mother's flight from Seattle. And perhaps they'll forget someday that there ever was a time when they didn't know why I was here.

"Do you suppose Doug knows I don't live with my father anymore?" Colleen asks.

I grin. "I think you'd better cross Doug's name off your list of friends."

"Why?"

"The only thing in the world that your father and Grandmother would ever agree on is that Doug is too cool a dude for you."

Colleen bends close to me. "Will we ever get to sit in the dining room with the grown-ups?"

I shrug, but I'm remembering how childish my mother thinks I am. "When do people grow up?" I ask.

❧ *Chapter 16* ❧

The movie Aaron takes me to isn't fun. It's violent and noisy, and one of the characters looks so much like the boy in San Francisco who calls himself Dancer that I close my eyes sometimes, or look away.

Something occurs to me, and I'm embarrassed with my secret discovery about myself. That dark dancer is so different from quiet, serious Aaron that I wonder if I was fascinated for more reasons than his appearance — and his street-corner business. I criticized Colleen for her interest in Doug. What would she think if she knew I'd gone back again to search for the exotic boy?

Had I been trying to get even with Aaron — with everyone — for Belle's matchmaking? And I was showing off, of course. I didn't want the boy to think I was a stupid tourist.

I'm so miserable that I can't sit still, and Aaron asks if I want to leave.

I'm not certain what I should do. He might be enjoying the movie — and he paid for my ticket. I sit undecided and miserable. At last I ask, "Do you like this?"

He glances at the screen, then at me. "I wouldn't fall over dead if you wanted to go," he whispers.

I laugh out loud. *Shhhhh,* everybody around hisses. *Shhhhh.*

We hurry out, saving the rest of our laughter as if it were candy until we're free of the theater.

"You should have said something right away," Aaron tells me. "We'd have left before you were grossed out by it."

"You could have asked for your money back," I say.

"Will they really give it to you?" he asks.

"Once Grandmother got ours back. She told the manager that she didn't want to spend money giving herself a nervous breakdown since ordinary life will take care of that if you don't initiate vigorous steps to prevent it."

Aaron laughs. "That sounds like something she'd say. She's great. I really like her."

But do you like me? I wonder.

We wander around the mall until it closes, then Aaron takes me to an old-fashioned ice-cream store where we sit at rickety little tables with wire legs and order banana splits. While we're waiting to be served, Aaron says that he misses Olivia.

"She used to come out and watch me for a few minutes every morning," he says. "She remembered when my dad painted the house, and she said I was doing just as good a job. I don't think that's true, but I appreciated hearing it."

I fiddle with my napkin and the clasp on my purse and the ends of my hair. I wish he wouldn't talk about Olivia, not after what Dr. Clement said today. Did Aaron hear? I don't dare ask.

"You've been through a lot," Aaron says. "I guess that's why you're so old for your age."

"Thank you, but it's not true. But I'll be fifteen in July," I tell him. "Then I'll only be a year younger than you."

"I'll be seventeen in October," he says. "Then we're back to where we started. But you'll still seem — I don't know. You don't go all to pieces over things."

I gawk at him. Doesn't he remember when I bawled all over him and he had to keep patting me and saying, "Sorry, sorry," so I wouldn't howl like Ben? I decide not to remind him. At this point in my life, I can use all the compliments I can get.

"So your friend will be living with you after this," he says to fill in the silence.

"Colleen? I hope so."

Our banana splits come and we eat without talking. I wonder if he's going to kiss me when we get home. And I'm worrying, too. I don't think he should. It's not such a good idea, all things considered. Grandmother wouldn't like it if she knew. Belle would tease me. And Colleen might laugh.

But — *But!* I wish he would.

It's still light when we get home. Aaron asks if he can sit on the porch for a while with me. I nod, hoping nobody heard us drive up. But Ben sticks his head out the screen door, sees Aaron, and gallops around like an idiot, barking.

Colleen comes out. "Do you two want something to eat?" she asks. "Minette made cherry cobbler."

"That sounds good," Aaron says. He's got a huge appetite.

We end up in the kitchen with everybody else, and the question of whether or not Aaron will kiss me is resolved. He won't. Not this time.

He leaves at nine-thirty. Belle goes to bed, Grandmother shuts herself up in her little office, Minette cleans the kitchen, and Yolande paces back and forth between the dollhouse and the porch, thinking, talking to herself. She's getting back into her book, and now things will go better for her.

Colleen and I sit on the porch swing and prop our feet on chairs. "How was your date?" she asks.

"The movie was awful but the banana splits were good."

"Did he ask you to go out with him again?"

I give her a look. "Are you kidding? In front of everybody?"

"You're right," Colleen says. "Well, it's not as if you don't see him nearly every day. At least until he's

174

finished painting the house. I'll probably never see Dangerous Doug again."

"Right," I say, but I can't laugh about it, not this time. A dark, graceful figure struts across my imagination, twirls, laughs.

Colleen sighs a great big sigh. "Oh, well. Doug was really only useful as a way of griping my father. And I think moving in here is an even better way."

I don't respond. I think about the afternoon argument again, and what her father said about Belle.

Why doesn't Colleen bring that up? She must have understood exactly what went on here the night Olivia died. Why doesn't she say something? Should I?

"I didn't thank you for what you said this afternoon," I tell her. "About me sitting with Olivia when . . ." I stop.

Colleen won't look at me. "I know what could have happened if you'd been home. So it might just as well have really happened."

Silence. "But . . ." I begin.

"Let it alone, Gray," she says. "Just let it alone. Don't talk about it again for a long time."

Ah, I think. Then she's caught on that we must wait until a safe time before we talk about some things. Only then can we tell the stories over and over until they don't hurt us so much anymore.

Suddenly I'm at peace about Olivia. Her way of leaving will be protected by us. I bet she knew she could trust us.

During the first two weeks of July, Grandmother and her lawyers haggle with Dr. Clement about Colleen. I worry that he might threaten us about Olivia again, but instead, he brings up the lease on his offices and this enrages Grandmother and Colleen.

"I'm being sold to your grandmother for a ten-year lease," Colleen says bitterly.

"She considers it cheap at the price," I say. "It's the principle of the thing that makes her so mad."

Nothing is decided. Dr. Clement is a master at keeping people in suspense, Colleen says.

"Grandmother's a master at making people sorry they tried it," I say. "And remember, now the social worker hates your father."

Aaron's father goes back to the hospital, and Aaron doesn't come to paint for several days. I miss him and finally phone him.

"Gee," he says. "Gee. Thanks for calling."

My left hand, holding the phone, tingles.

When Aaron returns to work, he's whistling. "My dad is coming home tomorrow," he says. He touches my shoulder and grins.

Then the house is finished, and so is the dollhouse and the garage. All that remains are the summer kitchen and the toolsheds at the end of the garden.

One afternoon Aaron, nursing a bee sting, sits on the porch with us drinking lemonade. "I'm going to give up on the summer kitchen," he says. "Your grandmother told me it'll be all right if I come back in the fall, after the honeysuckle quits blooming and the bees are gone." I don't dare smile — after all, he just got stung — but I'm glad he'll still be coming around when summer's over. Maybe, just maybe, he'll take me out again. I can't think past that.

Colleen's birthday is on July twenty-first and mine is on the twenty-seventh. We have a joint celebration dinner downtown with Grandmother, Minette, Yolande, Belle — and Belle's darling old dentist.

"He's got a crush on her," Colleen whispers to me while we're waiting for our salads.

She's right, and they're cute together. Belle is happier now than we've seen her since Olivia died.

But I'm wrong. The next day she's limping and massaging her hands again, her face drawn with pain. Rain falls all afternoon, not a warm honeysuckle rain, but a nasty one from the north, so cold that Grandmother turns on the furnace.

"I hate this climate," Belle says. "I was born here, but I hate the cold rains. And winter's coming again. It seems that spring just got here. I must be getting old." She's restless, too. Colleen and I hear her moving around at night. I tell Grandmother, and she says that Belle's arthritis keeps her awake.

On the last day of July, Dr. Clement agrees to let Colleen stay with us. At a separate meeting, Grandmother agrees to renew his lease, but only for three years. He may not know it, but she's planning on throwing him out when Colleen's eighteen.

"He'll be out on his ass," Colleen crows. She's beginning to sound like Belle. Grandmother shakes her head but I laugh.

And also on the last day of July, Aaron finishes painting everything but the summer kitchen. To celebrate both events, Grandmother invites Aaron to dinner and Minette spends all afternoon cooking. But Belle phones from the hospital and tells us that she won't be here.

"Why not?" Colleen demands of us. "This is the most important day of my life. My mother's coming! How can Belle not come home?"

Grandmother, looking worried, makes small healing remarks, but Colleen's feelings are hurt. And I'm scared. Belle looked so strange this morning before she left. I thought then that something was going on, something she didn't want us to know about.

Lucy, Colleen's mother, arrives early, looking years younger and happier than I've ever seen her. Aaron goes home and comes back dressed up. When Minette announces that dinner is ready, the whole crowd looks absolutely wonderful.

Everybody toasts everybody else with water, and we laugh all through the meal. The house looks beautiful, Colleen is safe, and Lucy can come visit whenever she wants.

"I wish Olivia could have seen this," Minette says. No one's eyes fill with tears. We all nod, even Aaron.

Bravely, I say, "I bet she knows all about it."

The dinner would be perfect if Belle were here. But

she doesn't come until we're having dessert, she and her admirer, the retired dentist.

"I have an announcement," she says, serious and scowling in the doorway. "I'm going to marry this fool next week, and we're moving to Hawaii."

Belle's wedding takes place on the porch one August afternoon. Cornelius mowed the lawn early, and for the rest of my life I'll think of the scents of fresh-cut grass and honeysuckle whenever I remember Belle.

Now there will be two empty chairs at teatime. I whisper this to Belle, and she hugs me hard.

After the reception, while the rest of us are clearing the dining room table, Belle says, "Garnet, this room's going to be so empty during teatime that you'll be able to raise an echo."

Grandmother, looking up from the tray of silverware, smiles at Belle. "I was thinking that myself."

Belle slips one arm around Colleen and the other around me. "Here are the women to fill the empty chairs," she says. "Just so the circle won't be broken."

Colleen and I look at each other and grin — but with great dignity, as befits *women*.

Summer is over. School starts in another week. Aaron and a friend of his are taking Colleen and me to a church dance near his house tonight. While I help Grandmother get tea ready, Colleen is upstairs trying one new hairdo after another.

"I hope this boy is nice," I say.

"If he's a friend of Aaron's, he must be," Grandmother says. "He'll be better for Colleen than that other one. What did Belle call him? A cool what?"

"Dude, Grandmother," I say, grinning. "A cool dude."

"Ugh," Grandmother says.

The clocks call out that it's four o'clock. "Ready?" Grandmother asks as she puts the teapot on the cart.

I slip the last of the cookies I baked on the plate. "Almost," I say.

Grandmother looks around. "What's missing?"

"Nothing except an explanation," I say. "Tell me why you broke off the hands on the clocks."

She shakes her head. "Why on earth are you bringing that up?"

"It's *time*," I say, laughing.

"Oh, all right." She drops a towel over the teapot to keep it warm. "But I should have made you figure it out yourself. Life can get so complicated. All I could ever manage was the twenty-four hours in a day. I believe I'd have lost my mind if I'd gone on worrying about the minutes, especially when your grandfather was so sick. To me, each hour is like a pocket. It can contain a little trouble or a lot. Or laughter. Or even embarrassment."

I nod. I know about embarrassment.

"Meals fit nicely in an hour," she goes on. "And a good visitor doesn't stay much longer. An hour is neat and tidy, do you see? Even during the worst of my problems, I know when I hear the clocks strike that some of the trouble is over, captured in that hour, and pretty soon I can link all the hours together, find the beginning and the end, and somehow the pain is contained."

"Then it's a teatime story," I say.

"Exactly."

"It's sort of like catching the honeysuckle rain," I say. "Some people hate rain in summer, but we collect it and use it for something good."

Grandmother nods. "Any kind of trouble, once you've contained it, can be put to use."

She laughs. "Rinsing your hair in honeysuckle water — learning about life from stories — in this house absolutely nothing goes to waste."

Yolande sticks her head around the corner. "Where's tea? We're famished." Ben makes desperate mooing sounds, slobbering in anticipation of cookies.

Grandmother pushes in the cart and I follow, to take the place at the table once occupied by Olivia. Colleen already sits in Belle's chair.

"Gray, did you make those cookies from Olivia's recipe?" she asks. "Hurry up and pass the plate. My stomach thinks my throat's been cut." And she barks a laugh the way Belle would have done.

Minette waves a postcard. "Did all of you see this? Belle says she's taking hula lessons."

"I believe it," Grandmother says, pouring tea into the cups. "Nothing Belle does can surprise me."

I pull out the note I received from Mother today.

"My mother's going to Hawaii on business and she says she'll spend a day or two with Belle."

"Norah's traveling again?" Yolande asks. "Fun for her. But she's awfully good at doing things on her own. I'm not, that's for certain. Remember all the trouble I got into when I went to Rome? I'm so half-witted I'll trust anybody."

Now is the time, I think. Grandmother has handed me my tea, so I take a sip.

"It's just as well that I'm not living with Mother," I say, more comfortable about what's coming than I thought I'd be. But then, I'm telling my story to women who've made mistakes, too. And they've been frightened and embarrassed at the results.

"I guess I've got the same problem Yolande has. Send me out on my own and the first thing I do is make eye contact with the worst person around."

And so I tell them about the strange dark dancer who intrigued me, tempted me, then terrified me. They're suitably astonished, a little worried, and finally amused. My tale has a beginning, a middle, and an end. I am, after all, one of the women at my grandmother's tea table, and how could I not be a storyteller?